Fiasco
by

Kathi Daley

This book is a work of fiction. Names, characters, places, and incidents either are products of the author's imagination or are used fictitiously. Any resemblance to actual events or locales or persons, living or dead, is entirely coincidental.

Copyright © 2018 by Katherine Daley

Version 1.0

I want to thank the very talented Jessica Fischer for the cover art.

I so appreciate Bruce Curran, who is always ready and willing to answer my cyber questions; Jayme Maness for helping out with the book clubs; and Peggy Hyndman for helping sleuth out those pesky typos.

And, of course, thanks to the readers and bloggers in my life, who make doing what I do possible.

Thank you to Randy Ladenheim-Gil for the editing.

And finally, I want to thank my husband Ken for allowing me time to write by taking care of everything else.

Books by Kathi Daley

Come for the murder, stay for the romance

Zoe Donovan Cozy Mystery:

Halloween Hijinks
The Trouble With Turkeys
Christmas Crazy
Cupid's Curse
Big Bunny Bump-off
Beach Blanket Barbie
Maui Madness
Derby Divas
Haunted Hamlet
Turkeys, Tuxes, and Tabbies
Christmas Cozy
Alaskan Alliance
Matrimony Meltdown
Soul Surrender
Heavenly Honeymoon
Hopscotch Homicide
Ghostly Graveyard
Santa Sleuth
Shamrock Shenanigans
Kitten Kaboodle
Costume Catastrophe
Candy Cane Caper
Holiday Hangover
Easter Escapade
Camp Carter
Trick or Treason
Reindeer Roundup
Hippity Hoppity Homicide

Firework Fiasco
Henderson House – *August 2018*

Zimmerman Academy The New Normal
Ashton Falls Cozy Cookbook

Tj Jensen Paradise Lake Mysteries by Henery Press:

Pumpkins in Paradise
Snowmen in Paradise
Bikinis in Paradise
Christmas in Paradise
Puppies in Paradise
Halloween in Paradise
Treasure in Paradise
Fireworks in Paradise
Beaches in Paradise – *July 2018*

Whales and Tails Cozy Mystery:

Romeow and Juliet
The Mad Catter
Grimm's Furry Tail
Much Ado About Felines
Legend of Tabby Hollow
Cat of Christmas Past
A Tale of Two Tabbies
The Great Catsby
Count Catula
The Cat of Christmas Present
A Winter's Tail
The Taming of the Tabby
Frankencat

The Cat of Christmas Future
Farewell to Felines
A Whisker in Time – *September 2018*

Writers' Retreat Southern Seashore Mystery:

First Case
Second Look
Third Strike
Fourth Victim
Fifth Night
Sixth Cabin
Seventh Chapter – *August 2018*

Rescue Alaska Paranormal Mystery:

Finding Justice
Finding Answers
Finding Courage - *September 2018*

A Tess and Tilly Mystery:

The Christmas Letter
The Valentine Mystery
The Mother's Day Mishap
The Halloween House – *July 2018*

Haunting by the Sea:
Homecoming by the Sea
Secrets by the Sea – *June 2018*

Sand and Sea Hawaiian Mystery:
Murder at Dolphin Bay
Murder at Sunrise Beach
Murder at the Witching Hour
Murder at Christmas
Murder at Turtle Cove
Murder at Water's Edge
Murder at Midnight

Seacliff High Mystery:
The Secret
The Curse
The Relic
The Conspiracy
The Grudge
The Shadow
The Haunting

Road to Christmas Romance:
Road to Christmas Past

Chapter 1

Thursday, July 5

"Elvis is dead."

I raised a brow and took a moment to consider whether my husband, Zak Zimmerman's honorary grandmother, Nona might have been hitting the bottle earlier than usual today. "Yes, I know. He's actually been dead for quite some time."

"Not that Elvis." Nona groaned in frustration. "A different Elvis. My Elvis didn't die on the bathroom floor, but on the bed I'd shared with him after I realized I'd had a bit too much of the juice to safely drive the bike back to your place."

By bike, I knew Nona meant her pink Harley, which she tended to drive like a woman with a death wish, and by juice, I knew she meant the whiskey she seemed to consider a food group. I wasn't sure I even wanted to know the details at this point, but Nona was

Zak's grandmother, and she appeared to be honestly rattled, so I took a deep breath and jumped in. "Maybe you should sit down and tell me everything. Start at the beginning."

Nona looked around the reception area of Zoe's Zoo, the wild and domestic rescue and rehabilitation center I own and help operate with my manager, Jeremy Fisher, who was out on paternity leave. "Sit where?"

"Charlie will show you to my office while I let Aspen know what we're doing."

Charlie was my Tibetan terrier. He came to the Zoo with me pretty much every time I was in, so when I told him to take Nona to the office, he knew just where to go. Once Nona and Charlie had gone down the hallway, I started back to the wild animal wing, where my newest employee, Aspen Wood, was cleaning the large pen where we kept the orphaned and injured bear cubs we were rehabilitating.

"Did I hear Nona's bike roll up?" Aspen asked.

"You did. She seems to have a problem she needs to discuss, so we'll be in my office. I'll leave a note telling anyone who comes in to ring the bell. I shouldn't have a problem hearing it and responding, but you might want to keep an ear out as well."

"No problem. In fact, once I'm finished here, I'll head up to the front and work on the flyers for the adoption clinic next month."

"Thanks, Aspen. You've been a real trooper, making sure everything is covered while both Jeremy and Tiffany are off for an extended period."

Aspen smiled. "It's not a problem, really. I love working here. Most of the time, there's nowhere I'd rather be."

I'd been very lucky to run into Aspen when I did. I'd first met her a couple of years ago, during an investigation regarding the death of a kitten mill owner. Aspen was an extremely vocal local activist who'd had run-ins with the deceased on more than one occasion, making her one of the top suspects in the woman's murder. While things had worked out in the end, I'd spent quite a lot of time looking into Aspen's activities as well as her past. What I'd found was a gentle soul who really cared about the animals she championed.

Once I left the note, I headed to my office, where Nona was chatting with Charlie. Sweet thing that he is, Charlie appeared to be listening to Nona's tale of too much whiskey, too much fun, and a dead Elvis she had no idea how to deal with.

"Okay, I should be able to give you my full attention now." I took the chair behind my desk. "I need you to tell me what happened from the time you left the group last evening until now."

Nona nodded. "Okay. I'll tell you what I can. I should warn you, though, that things are pretty blurry after a certain point."

"Just do the best you can."

Nona lifted her head of white hair and looked me in the eye before she began. "As you know, I attended the annual Fourth of July fireworks celebration with you and the family last night. Afterward, you all decided to go home to put the kids to bed, but I was feeling pretty wound up after the festivities, so I decided to head over to my favorite bar for a drink or two. It was at the bar that I met Elvis."

I held up my hand. "Let me stop you right there. Was this guy named Elvis or did he look like Elvis?"

"I have no idea what the guy's real name was or what he looked like when he wasn't in costume. He was in town with eleven other Elvis impersonators for the contest Dirk Pendleton is running."

I seemed to remember something about Hollywood heartthrob and part-time Ashton Falls resident Dirk Pendleton opening a casino in Reno. I was pretty sure he planned to go with a fifties and sixties theme and name the place Shake Rattle and Roll. I'd also heard he was lining up impersonators of all the greats of the eras, including Elvis Presley. He'd been holding competitions around the country to choose these impersonators as a publicity stunt. "Let me guess. Dirk Pendleton is holding his competition for the official Elvis impersonator for Shake Rattle and Roll here in Ashton Falls."

Nona nodded, confirming what I should already have known. Usually I was in the middle of whatever was going on in town, but I'd been so busy lately, I hadn't been paying a lot of attention to the local news.

"Why our little town? The competitions for the other impersonators have been held in large metropolitan areas."

"I don't know for certain, but maybe he wanted to hold at least one of the competitions in his sometime hometown. Do you really think this line of questioning is important? I did just tell you the man I spent the night with was deader than a doornail when I woke up this morning. Seems to me that would be the talking point we'd want to pursue."

Nona had a point. "Of course. Go on with your story."

"So anyway, I went to my usual bar and was drinking my usual whiskey when this bunch of men all dressed exactly like Elvis walked in. I didn't pay them much attention at first, but then one of them, dressed in a blue sequined outfit, came over to the bar where I was sitting and asked if he could buy me a drink. Never one to turn down a free drink, I agreed. At first, I found the costume ridiculous, but the longer I talked with the guy, the easier it was for me to let my imagination take over. At some point I let myself believe it was the real Elvis, and when he suggested we move to a table where we could get to know each other, I agreed. I excused myself to use the ladies' room shortly after we moved to a table. When I came out my Elvis was chatting with another one, who happened to be wearing white leather from head to foot. The man in white, who I learned was dumber than a chicken without a head and was referred to as Elvis #7, invited my Elvis, who was Elvis #3, to a party on the beach. I was really in to the whole vibe of the evening, so I agreed to go."

I waited as Nona paused before continuing. It amazed me that she had so much energy for a woman of her age. Heck, she could outparty a woman of any age. It had been a long time since I'd pulled an all-nighter.

"Anyway," Nona went on, "we all headed down to the beach. One of the Elvises, I think Elvis #11, had a keg, and another had a cooler of rum punch. A couple of the guys had brought illegal fireworks and were shooting them off over the water. There was a huge bonfire going on, and everyone seemed to be having a good time. At least until my Elvis, Elvis #3, tried to set off some sort of rocket-looking thing, got lined up wrong, and ended up shooting directly toward one of the other Elvises. This, of course, started a war of sorts, in which the Elvises divided into two teams and began shooting these rockets at one another." Nona chuckled. "With all those wigs and all those fancy duds to catch fire, it was a tragedy waiting to happen."

"Not to mention the risk of a forest fire," I added. "There's a reason fireworks other than the show put on by the town are illegal in Ashton Falls."

Nona nodded. "Yeah, I guess there's that as well."

"So back to your involvement with Elvis #3..." I said persuasively.

"The rocket war got pretty heated, and the next thing I knew fists were flying and the Elvises all started punching one another. My Elvis didn't want to ruin his very expensive costume, so he suggested we take the party somewhere else. He didn't have a car, so he rode with me on my hog. I'm still not sure how I ended up back at his room, but he had plenty of whiskey, and we were having a good time, so I didn't resist the idea when he suggested it. I didn't intend to spend the entire night with the guy, but it got late and I started to feel dizzy, so I decided it wasn't a good idea to drive. At some point I guess I passed out. When I woke up this morning Elvis was lying on top of the covers fully clothed, the same as me. Unlike me, however, Elvis was dead."

"So, are we thinking the guy had partied a bit too much, bringing on a heart attack?"

Nona shook her head. "No, not a heart attack. Someone stuck a big ol' knife in his chest."

"A knife?" I asked. "He was stabbed in the chest with a knife?"

Nona frowned at me. "You need to learn to pay more attention when folks are talking. I just said the man had a knife in his chest."

"And you have no idea how it got there?"

Nona shook her head once again. "Not a clue. I'll admit it was kind of odd that a man could have been stabbed to death on the opposite side of the bed from where I was sleeping without me waking up."

My brows furrowed. "Odd isn't exactly the word I'd use. Are you sure you don't remember hearing or seeing anyone come in?"

"I'm sure. The last thing I remember was Elvis turning on the television. I decided to lay down for just a minute to see if the dizziness would go away. The next thing I knew, it was morning and Elvis was dead."

Okay, Zoe. Don't freak out. I'm sure this isn't as bad as it sounds. Just take a deep breath and try to figure out what to do next. "So, what exactly does the sheriff think happened?"

Nona shrugged. "As far as I know, he doesn't know a thing about any of this."

"You didn't call 911 when you realized Elvis had been murdered?"

"'Course not. The fuzz are going to think I did it. When I woke up and saw Elvis I came straight over here. I didn't touch anything or talk to anyone. You have to help me. No one is going to believe I slept right through a murder."

Nona made another good point. Even if she'd drunk a lot you'd think a man being stabbed to death would be a noisy enough event to wake even the drunkest individual. "Okay. Let's go over to the motel where you left Elvis. We'll assess the situation and then call Salinger. He'll know what to do."

"Sheriff Salinger isn't in town."

I frowned. "What do you mean, he isn't in town?"

"I got pulled over for going fifty in a twenty-five. I guess I might have said some disrespectful things to the young'un, who didn't look old enough to shave, let alone be a cop. Guess he took offense, because he threatened to arrest me for reckless driving. I tried to tell the punk that I was good friends with Sherriff Salinger and that if he just called him, he'd vouch for me, but the kid told me Salinger was off finding himself and he was filling in."

Oh, that wasn't good. Not good at all. Sherriff Salinger and I had become good friends after a rocky start years ago. I'd helped him out and he'd helped me. He knew Nona, quirks and all, and most likely would have given her the benefit of the doubt. But some new deputy just starting out and most likely looking for that one case that would help to put his name on the map? A dead Elvis found lying on the bed next to a Harley-riding, free-loving, heavy-drinking grandma would be just the thing a young deputy would love to sink his claws in to. Add to the mix the fact that the very popular Dirk Pendleton was the one sponsoring the contest and you had just the sort of news item that made it to national platforms. There was no doubt about it: If what Nona said was true, we were going to have to deal with the specifics of the situation very carefully indeed.

******

The Nickelodeon was a midrange motel with a decent reputation smack dab in the middle of town. Nona had left the Do Not Disturb sign on the door so the maid wouldn't think the room was empty and wander in. She'd kept the key so we'd be able to get back in when we arrived. I felt my stomach knot as Nona opened the door. If Nona had been a witness to a death, even an unconscious one, we needed to tell someone what we knew.

"Well, that's odd," Nona said.

I entered the room behind her. It was empty. I mean, completely empty. And it had been cleaned. There was no visible evidence that anyone had ever been there. "Are you sure this is the right room?"

"I'm sure. Number fourteen." Nona held up the key. "I have the key to room fourteen and it opened the door. Maybe the maid came in, even though I left the Do Not Disturb sign on the door. Maybe the motel manager called the cops and they came and took the body away."

"No," I answered. "If the sheriff's office was called in response to a murder this whole area would be taped off. If there actually was a dead man in this room someone else moved him, then cleaned things up."

"*If* there was a dead man in this room? Are you doubting me?"

"You did say you were drunk enough to pass out," I reminded Nona.

"I may have been drunk last night, but I wasn't drunk when I woke up this morning."

"Maybe you were groggy after your long night," I suggested. "I know I'm pretty much worthless until I have my second cup of coffee. Ask Zak; he'll tell you."

"I wasn't groggy. I didn't imagine that the man I spent the night with was dead. I'm telling you, I know what I saw. The guy was lying right here with a knife through his chest. The bed was covered with blood. His blood."

I pulled back the covers. "It looks fine now."

Nona rolled her eyes. "Obviously, someone cleaned the room and changed the sheets."

I wanted to believe Nona. Strike that: I *didn't* want to believe Nona. I hoped with all my might that she'd been hungover and maybe a bit delirious, or perhaps age had finally caught up with her and she'd simply forgotten what she'd seen. Maybe a man had been stabbed in the movie they'd watched last night and she'd dreamed about it. Or perhaps she was making this whole thing up to get back at me for suggesting she might be getting a bit too old to go running around the country on a pink Harley.

"I can prove it," Nona said when I didn't answer for a while.

"How?"

"We'll go to the Elvis competition. Instead of twelve contestants, there'll be eleven. Not only will that prove my Elvis was murdered while I slept, but we'll be able to find out who the guy really was."

I supposed it couldn't hurt to head over to the competition. Even if there was a missing Elvis, that didn't prove he was murdered while lying two feet away from Nona, but if all the Elvises were accounted for it did suggest Nona was mistaken and no one had died. I used my phone and took as many photos of the room as I could from every angle before we left. If there was a missing Elvis the photos could provide us with a clue to help solve the case, should we at some point lose access to the room. Boy, I sure hoped Dirk had all twelve of his Elvises accounted for.

Chapter 2

Dirk had built a bandstand on the beach near the north end of the lake. The competition was to take place over a long weekend when all twelve contestants would be provided the opportunity to mingle with the celebrity judges and to perform individually. I was sure Dirk was looking for a spokesperson who not only looked like the King himself but was personable and an excellent performer. In my opinion, it seemed like a lot of trouble to go through for a small theme casino, but what did I know?

I'd insisted on driving my car and had somehow persuaded Nona to leave her Harley at the Zoo. The weekend event was to kick off later that afternoon with a group production where all twelve impersonators would be introduced, giving each the opportunity to charm the crowd and the judges. Later that evening there would be a concert during which all twelve men would perform a song made famous by the real Elvis back in the day.

"It looks like there's an information booth over near the entrance to the bleachers," I said after taking a minute to get the lay of the land. "Maybe they'll have a program or something that lists all the contestants. That will help us to find out the real name of the Elvis you found dead in his bed."

The information booth wasn't staffed at the moment because the introductions wouldn't begin for another two hours, but I spotted a poster on the wall with photos of all twelve Elvises and their names and occupations.

"That's him." Nona pointed to Elvis #3. "Calvin Jobs. An insurance salesman and former Elvis impersonator from Las Vegas, Nevada." Nona glanced at me. "Somehow knowing that kills the fantasy."

"A man is dead, or at least according to what you think you saw, a man is dead. I think the time for fantasy is over."

"I know what I saw," Nona insisted. "What do we do now?"

"We need to find out whether Elvis #3 is alive and kicking or boots up, as you suspect. We could just wait for the introduction ceremony that's taking place in two hours' time, but I'm thinking maybe Ashton Falls' new events coordinator, Hillary Spain, might have a contact that can get us the information sooner. She isn't in charge of this event because it's been privately planned and funded, but Dirk would have needed a permit to hold it on the beach, so I'm sure she found a way to poke her finger into the pie."

"I thought you were a member of that committee."

"I was. I took some time off when I had Catherine. I plan to return in the fall if my mom can watch her for a couple of hours every Wednesday morning."

I pulled out my cell and called Hillary, who was a nice-enough person, although, like Willa, the woman she replaced, she was a stickler for the rules. In the beginning I was afraid her lack of experience in our community was going to be a problem for someone who tended to wing it in those instances when she didn't know the correct ordinance to be adhered to, but as time passed and she began to grow into her job, I could see she was going to do fine.

"Hillary, it's Zoe Zimmerman," I said when she answered. "I was wondering if you had a contact in the Elvis competition."

"Dirk Pendleton filed for all the proper permits, but he made it clear he didn't need any help with the organization and implementation of the show. Why do you ask?"

"I need to track down one of the Elvises and hoped you might have someone who could help me do it."

"Why don't you just ask your husband?"

"My husband?"

"I happen to know he met with Dirk several times in the weeks prior to the committee granting the permit to hold the competition on the beach. From what I could see, the two of them were pretty buddy-buddy."

Zak knew Dirk from a prior investigation, when the Easter Bunny robbed the bank, and he continued to attend event committee meetings after I'd decided to take some time off. Zak was an educated, professional, sophisticated, and extremely likable guy. I supposed it made sense that he would be the one to work with one of Hollywood's biggest heartthrobs on behalf of the town. "I didn't realize Zak had worked on that project. With a new baby in the house, there isn't always time to catch up on the day-to-day details of our lives. "I'll ask him about it. Thanks."

As soon I hung up, Nona began shaking her head. "No, no, no. We can't tell Zak what's going on."

"Why not?" I asked. "He might be able to help."

"Zak is my little buggy boo. I don't want him to know what a mess I've made of things."

Buggy boo? I'd never in all the years I'd known Nona heard her use baby talk to communicate with or describe anyone. Maybe she really was losing it. "Okay," I said. "We won't tell him what's going on for now. But if it turns out there really has been a murder we have to tell him everything."

Nona looked like she was going to argue.

"Everything," I said again.

"Oh, okay," Nona growled. "He'll find out eventually anyway." Nona's facial expression faded from moderately angry to completely befuddled.

"What?" I asked.

"Elvis's room. It was completely clean, as if no one had ever been there."

"That's right," I agreed. "I was there."

"Today's the first day of the contest. The rooms for the contestants have been booked through Sunday, yet there were no personal items in that one. If I had simply dreamed the whole dead-man-in-the-bed thing and Elvis really hadn't been murdered, where was his stuff? I remember he had at last three large suitcases."

"Good point," I admitted. "I suppose we can ask whether he checked out or anyone checked him out."

"Do you think the motel manager will give you that information?"

I shrugged. "He might. I guess it depends who's on desk duty. We don't have a contact to ask if Elvis #3 still plans to go on, so we might as well head back to the motel to see what we can find out there."

As it had before, Nona's keycard opened the door of room fourteen. It was still immaculate and completely devoid of personal possessions. I headed to the office to see what I could find out, while Nona waited in the room. If she'd been seen in Elvis's company the previous evening and he did turn out to have been murdered, I didn't want to strengthen the link between them in anyone's mind until we had the opportunity to figure this out.

Luckily for me, the man working the counter today had been a regular at the diner my best friend Ellie Denton owned before it burned down.

"Zoe. How have you been?" David Dugan asked.

"I've been good."

"Heard you had a baby."

I nodded. "A daughter. Catherine. She's six months old and the cutest thing you'll ever see."

"I bet. I'd like to meet her sometime. 'Course, now that Ellie has a young'un of her own and doesn't work in the restaurant business, I rarely run into either of you."

"Ellie and I will stop by with the babies when we're in town sometime," I promised. "Listen, I'm looking for the guy in room fourteen. His name is

Calvin Jobs and he's here for the Elvis impersonator competition. I stopped by his room, but it was empty. Did he check out?"

"Nope. All twelve rooms booked by the impersonators were paid for through Monday. He might be out on the beach for the event. I can leave a message for him if you'd like."

"No, that's fine. I'll just track him down there." I turned to go, then turned back around. "I understand some of the Elvises partied pretty hard last night. Any noise complaints?"

David shook his head. "No. Things were pretty quiet as far as I know. My shift ended at eight, but the graveyard clerk didn't mention any problems. I imagine if the impersonators were looking to tie one on they went to a bar. Seems like with the fireworks show everyone was in town. Did Catherine enjoy her first July Fourth celebration?"

"She slept through the whole thing, but Ellie's son, Eli, loved every minute of it. I can't wait until next year when Catherine's a little older. How old is your son now?"

"I have a four year old and a six year old. Both kids oohed and aahed at every colorful explosion. It seems like the town really outdid itself this year."

"Yeah. It was an excellent show. It was good seeing you."

"Don't forget to stop by with the baby."

"I won't."

I returned to room fourteen to find Nona sitting on the edge of the bed with a look that reminded me of a lost child's on her face. I sat down beside her and took her hand in mine. "Don't worry. We'll figure this out."

Nona patted my hand. "I know we will. I just feel so bad for that poor man. I just can't imagine what could have happened that would have led to his death. And I really can't think how I could have slept through the whole thing. If I had woken up maybe I could have helped him."

"Or maybe you would have ended up dead as well." I bit my lower lip as I looked around the room. How on earth could a man have been stabbed to death without anyone hearing what was going on? The motel was fully occupied, so there must have been other guests on the premises when he was killed. You would think there would have been some sort of a ruckus, even if an attempt to protect himself had been futile. Nona said he'd been lying on the bed fully clothed, same as her. That told me that he'd passed out before he could change out of his Elvis costume. "You said you came back to the room last night and then began to feel dizzy. Do you remember if you had a drink after arriving here?"

"Elvis had a bottle of whiskey and offered me a drink. That rum punch at the beach was a little sweet for my taste and I never have been much of a beer drinker, so I was happy to have some of the good stuff to cleanse my pallet."

"Did Elvis have a drink from the same bottle?"

"No. He drank a beer instead."

"So it was after you drank the whiskey that you began to feel dizzy?" I verified.

"Yes. When we first got here I was feeling fine. After I had the whiskey I began to feel dizzy, so I lay down for a minute. I remember Elvis stretching out on the bed and reaching out for the remote control to turn on the television, and the next thing I knew, it was morning and Elvis was dead."

"I think you might have been drugged last night. That would explain why you didn't wake up even as the man in the bed beside you was being killed."

"You think Elvis drugged me? Why would he do that?"

I frowned. "I don't know. I suppose he might have planned on some sort of a date rape scenario."

Nona chuckled. "Honey, the man made me believe he was Elvis. A date rape drug wouldn't have been necessary to get me in the sack; if I stayed conscious, that is. No, I don't think that was the guy's intent. If he did drug me there must have been something else going on."

I tried to suppress the blush I couldn't quite control. Nona was a free-spirited hippie sort who I knew had an active sex life, but I didn't like to think about it and certainly didn't want to hear about the details. "Like what? I can't imagine what possible reason he would have had for drugging you, but it would explain a lot."

"Maybe, but my being drugged doesn't explain who would kill him or why. And it doesn't tell us where the body is now or how someone managed to clean up the room and move all the luggage with no one noticing anything."

"True, and the total time lapse between when you left the room and came to find me and we returned to the motel to find the body gone and the room clean was maybe ninety minutes. How could anyone completely remove all traces of a murder in only ninety minutes?"

"Maybe they didn't. Maybe we need one of those lights they use on TV. You know, the ones that show blood even when it's invisible to the naked eye."

If Salinger was in town I wouldn't hesitate to call him, and we'd do just that. But I hated to call the sheriff's office when a man I'd never met was in charge. At least not until I had to. If a murder was confirmed we'd make the call. In the meantime, it didn't make sense to do anything to bring Nona to his attention any more than she already was.

"You said there was blood on the bed," I said again.

"Yes. Both Elvis and I were lying on top of the bedspread when I woke up. There was a knife in his chest and a pool of blood under him."

"Did you notice anything else? Blood on the floor, or maybe blood spatter on the wall? Did the killer wash up in the bathroom perhaps?"

Nona got up and began to pace. "I don't remember seeing blood anywhere other than the bed, but I didn't take the time to look around. I saw Elvis was dead and I panicked. I ran out the door heading directly to the Zoo, which is where you told me yesterday you'd be today."

I pulled back the bedspread, the sheets, and the mattress pad. Not a sign of blood anywhere. Surely if a man was murdered on this bed there would be blood all the way down to the mattress. I supposed someone could have changed the bedding and flipped the mattress, but there was no way they were going to change out a mattress with no one noticing. "Help me flip this," I instructed.

Still no blood.

"Are you sure this is the right room?" I asked.

"It was number fourteen. I have the key to number fourteen. My key opened the door."

That was true. The key in Nona's possession had opened the door to room fourteen.

"Okay, let's head back to the competition. It's almost time for the opening ceremonies. We may as well find out if Elvis #3 is a go or a no-show."

Chapter 3

By the time we arrived at the beach, spectators were beginning to mill around. The gates had been opened and people were beginning to take seats in the bandstand. I'd hoped we'd be able to find out the status of Elvis #3 without waiting to watch the show, but it wasn't shaping up that way. I was about to give up and look for a seat when Dirk Pendleton himself walked toward us.

"If it isn't Zoe Zimmerman." Dirk took both my hands in his and kissed me on the cheek.

I was totally stunned that he remembered me from our brief meeting years ago. Sure, I'd fallen all over myself like a fangirl when Zak had introduced us, but I was sure he was used to that, so I didn't assume I'd made all that much of an impression. "It's good to see you too," I managed to stammer out, which was actually a miracle considering the first time we met I was so starstruck I couldn't put together a coherent sentence.

"And who is this lovely vision?" Dirk asked, taking Nona's hands in his.

I couldn't help but notice the heightened pink in Nona's complexion. "This is Zak's grandmother, Nona," I answered.

"Grandmother?" Dirk pretended not to believe my words. "There's no way this lovely young thing is anyone's grandmother!"

"Oh my, aren't you the charmer." Nona grinned from ear to ear.

Personally, I thought Dirk was laying it on a little too thick, but Nona was beaming, so I kept my mouth shut and grinned along with her.

"Are you here for the competition?" Dirk asked.

"We're here to support a friend," I answered, recognizing an in to the information I wanted. "Elvis #3, Calvin Jobs."

"Oh. I'm sorry to have to tell you this." Dirk's smiled faded just a bit. "I'm afraid Calvin had to drop out of the competition. I was sorry to hear it. I'd spoken to him on several occasions and felt he had real potential."

"Do you know why he dropped out?" I asked.

"One of the other Elvises, a man named Eric Spencer, told me that Calvin had a change of heart and just took off without even giving us enough notice to find a replacement. My event manager is livid, but I do understand stage fright, and how it can cripple a person."

"You think Calvin had stage fright?" I asked. I seemed to remember his bio said he'd worked in Vegas as an impersonator in the past, and he certainly hadn't gotten this far in the competition if he hadn't preformed before. The stage fright angle made no sense in my mind, and I was surprised Dirk believed it either.

"I'm sure of it. I happened to wander over to the stage during rehearsals yesterday and he was pacing around, talking to someone on the phone. I overheard him say that the stress was too much for him and he just couldn't follow through with his commitment. I'd noticed him fidgeting before one of the rehearsals and put two and two together. I was going to say something to him, but then one of the other contestants wandered over and I didn't want to embarrass him by saying I'd overheard his conversation. My heart goes out to the guy. It really does. When I first started in show business I was so terrified of going on stage that I threw up pretty much every time I had a live event."

"During?" I asked.

"No. Thankfully, the cookie toss was before I went on. It took me a long time to get to the point where the thought of a public appearance didn't cause a lot more stress than I wanted to deal with. I might have quit if it hadn't been for my father breathing down my neck, insisting I make something of myself."

Dirk was such a big star, I'd never thought of him having insecurities like the rest of us mere mortals. I wanted to grill him for more information about Elvis #3, but his event coordinator was waving him over, so he said good-bye and left.

"Now do you believe me?" Nona asked.

"I believe something is going on."

"So what now?"

Good question. I felt like I should call the man who was covering for Salinger, but really, what was I going to tell him? My husband's grandmother woke up next to a dead man, but all traces of him and the blood he'd shed were gone?

"We should tell Zak what's going on."

I could see Nona wasn't happy with that idea.

"It's either Zak or the guy filling in for Salinger. If Elvis #3 really is dead, we need to find out who killed him before the trail grows cold."

"Call the kid filling in for Salinger," Nona said. "If you tell Zak he'll just call the kid anyway, plus he'll know what a crazy old woman he has for a grandmother."

I picked up the phone to call the sheriff's office, even though I suspected that with absolutely zero proof as to what had occurred, the guy probably wouldn't believe us. Not that I'd blame him. The whole thing was too ridiculous to be real.

******

"Let me get this straight," the substitute deputy, whose name, we learned, was Buckner, said when Nona finished telling her story. "You met a man dressed as Elvis in a bar last night. You went with him back to his room, where you passed out. When you woke up this morning, you found the man lying in a pool of blood with a knife in his chest. You then hopped on your Harley and went to find Ms. Zimmerman."

"That's what I said."

"How old are you exactly?" he asked.

"It's not polite to ask a woman her age," Nona replied.

"Never mind." He typed something into the computer, then looked at the screen. He whistled. "Older than I would have guessed."

I cringed as I waited for Nona to belt him. If you wanted to live you needed to know that commenting on Nona's age wasn't good for your health. Thankfully, she decided to behave and simply glared at him. I didn't blame him; even I thought he was being a lot ruder than he needed to be.

"Are you going to look into this or not?" Nona demanded.

He let out a loud sigh. It was obvious he'd just as soon send us on our way, but I had to give him some credit when he got up, grabbed his car keys, and headed to the door. Nona and I followed him to the motel in my car. He took the key from Nona, then told us to wait in my car until he had a chance to check things out. After a few minutes he came out.

"There's no evidence anyone died in that room. Not recently, at least."

"I know what I saw," Nona insisted.

"I'm sure you do." He looked at me. "Can I speak to you for a moment, ma'am?"

I got out of the car and followed him a few steps away.

"I can't tell if this is just some huge joke you're playing on the new guy as retribution for pulling your grandmother over for speeding the other day, or if your grandmother needs to have her medication adjusted. I do know there's no way some guy was stabbed to death in that room less than twenty-four hours ago."

"I know how it looks and sounds, but Nona seems so sure, and Elvis #3 has pulled out of the competition. At least talk to the people over there to see what you can find out."

"Sounds like a huge waste of my time."

"Maybe, but it will help to put Nona's mind at ease. I mean, how hard could it be to track down this Calvin Jobs and have a chat with him? If you can confirm that he's alive and well that will be the end of it."

The man closed his eyes, let out a breath, and shook his head. "I'm more than certain this is a waste of time, but if it will make you happy I'll see what I can do. In return, you have to promise me that neither you nor your nona are going to run around town telling everyone that one of the Elvises was murdered in his room last night. You must know all that will accomplish is cause a lot of heartache for a lot of folks."

"I won't talk about it. Nona won't either." I would, however, I'd decided, tell Zak what was going on. It didn't feel right to keep it from him, despite Nona's request. Besides, chances were, he could help me make some sense of this mess.

******

I had to hand it to Zak: he managed to make it through Nona's explanation without a single look of doubt or disbelief. He sat quietly, giving her his full attention, asking reasonable questions, and offering thoughts of concern and sympathy where appropriate. The gentle approach he took toward the whole thing made me feel bad for all the times I'd thought Nona's sanity was in doubt.

"Don't worry, Nona." Zak wrapped his huge arms around the small woman who obviously meant a lot to him. "I'll take care of everything. All I need for you to do is to lay low until this is straightened out."

Fat chance of that happening, I thought to myself. Nona was the sort to fly high. Laying low never had been her style, at least since I'd known her. I first met Nona when she stayed with Zak and me in the days leading up to our wedding. Not only had she rolled into town on her pink Harley wearing a pink leather jacket, but when I found out she'd arrived I'd gone looking for her and found her doing yoga out by our pool. Totally naked.

According to the Zimmerman family, though, Nona had once been a rigid, controlling woman who lived to impose her will on others. She'd lived her life based on a stringent set of rules she enforced with an iron fist. Then she had a stroke and became a totally different person. The new and, I think, improved Nona doesn't seem to understand the boundaries most people live by. She does what she wants, when she wants, how she wants, with little regard to what anyone else might think about it. I do love her for that. I also worry about her for the same reason. She doesn't seem to understand that the laws of physics apply to her too, and she's just as likely to come to harm as anyone else. When she's in town I find myself worrying she'll drink too much, hook up with the wrong person, or crash the hog she rides. Having said that, I wouldn't change a single thing about her. Nona might not have a lot of years left, but you can be darn well certain she'll live them on her own terms.

Zak finished listening to everything Nona had to say, then sent her out to the pool to cool off after reminding her that children lived in our house, so a mandatory bathing suit policy would have to be enforced.

"What do you think?" I asked when we were alone.

"I'm not sure," Zak answered. "Nona believes she saw this man lying in a pool of blood with a knife in his chest. I'm convinced she's very sure of what she saw, and given the fact that the guy seems to have disappeared, I'm inclined to believe her. But if he died in that room I honestly can't believe there's absolutely no evidence to find."

"What if it was a hit carried out by the mob and they sent a cleaner to take care of things?" I said. "You know, like in that movie we watched."

Zak leaned forward and kissed me on the forehead. "While I value your idea, and agree that it might very well have merit, at this point my tendency is to think there's something simpler going on that we just haven't figured out yet."

"Yeah, probably. It seems to me that for everything to have played out the way Nona said it did, there had to have been several things going on. For one, it seems Nona was drugged. Why? If someone wanted Elvis dead, why not wait until she wasn't around? Drugging her and then killing him while she was in the room seems like a needless risk."

"Agreed."

"And then there's the fact that Nona was left as a witness of sorts," I continued. "Why would someone kill Elvis and then just leave her there in the bed, knowing she was sure to wake up and discover the body at some point? Seems like another needless risk."

"Or maybe it was part of the plan," Zak suggested.

"Part of the plan?" I lifted a brow. "How?"

"I'm not sure. I think the fact that Elvis was left for Nona to find was intentional."

"Okay, that's a frightening thought."

Zak wrapped his arms around me and pulled me into his chest. He held me tight, letting me find comfort in his embrace, until I heard Catherine fussing through the baby monitor. I kissed Zak quickly on the lips, then headed up to get her.

"Look who's awake," I greeted the suddenly smiling and happily squealing baby.

"Ma," Catherine crooned as I lifted her out of her crib and kissed her on top of her thick head of dark brown curls.

"Did Daddy take good care of you while I was gone?"

"Da." Catherine pulled a handful of my hair.

I laughed as I put her down on the changing table. After making sure she had a dry diaper and a fresh jumper, I picked her up and went downstairs. Sitting her in her high chair, I opened the refrigerator and took out a Tupperware container of homemade baby food. Not that I made it, mind you. Homemade baby food was more of a Zak thing.

"You're back early." Alex Bremmerton, one of the teenagers Zak and I were raising, walked in from the pool.

"I wasn't at the Zoo all that long. Aspen is covering while I look into a situation for Nona."

"A situation?" Alex took a bite of an apple she'd grabbed from a bowl on the table.

I know there are a lot of mothers out there who wouldn't tell their thirteen-year-old daughter that the woman she knew as an honorary grandmother had found a dead man in her bed after waking up in a motel room, but I wasn't one of those mothers; I caught her up on what had happened.

"Wow, poor Nona. When she came out to swim I thought she seemed a little deflated. She didn't even do her signature cannonball into the pool. As hard as it is to believe, she actually walked into the water down the steps on the shallow end."

"When she first told me what happened, she didn't seem overly upset, but I can see it's really starting to get to her. Maybe it's become more real to her as time passes."

"I'll try to cheer her up," Alex offered. She looked around the room. "Where's Charlie?"

My hand flew to my mouth. "Oh my gosh. Charlie! I left him with Aspen when Nona showed up. I should go." I glanced at Catherine.

"I'll feed her," Alex offered. "And after she eats I'll bring her out to the patio and put her in her bouncy chair. She loves to watch Scooter play in the pool."

"Thanks." I reached out and hugged Alex. "I'll let Zak know you have Catherine. I'll try to hurry."

"Take your time," Alex encouraged. "Catherine and I will be fine. Won't we, baby?"

Catherine screamed in response, which I assumed meant she was happy to spend time with her big sister.

Chapter 4

Thankfully, Charlie had been perfectly happy to spend the day with Aspen at the Zoo and had no idea I'd forgotten about him in all the confusion.

"I'm sorry I ended up being gone all day," I apologized to Aspen.

"Charlie and I were fine," Aspen responded. "Is Nona okay?"

"Not really. I'll tell you what's going on, but you have to promise not to tell anyone else. At least not until we figure things out."

"Of course," Aspen promised me.

I hopped up onto the counter and began my story. I could tell by the changing expressions on Aspen's face that she was as shocked by the tale as I'd been.

"Wow," she said when I was done. "What are you going to do?"

"I'm not sure yet. On one hand, figuring out what did or didn't happen to the man Nona knows as Elvis #3 isn't my job. We've notified the authorities, which pretty much passes the responsibility for solving the mystery to them. On the other hand, Nona is really upset. I have a feeling she won't be satisfied with leaving it alone. And maybe she shouldn't be. If a man *was* murdered, someone should be trying to figure out what happened to him."

"If you need me to work extra hours while you try to figure this out, don't worry about it," Aspen offered.

"Thanks. I'm going to try to juggle things so I can spend some of my time here at the Zoo. It's been a long time since I've helped out on any kind of a regular basis. I was actually looking forward to being here while Jeremy and Tiffany were off. But I know from experience that murder investigations have a way of taking over any schedule I might try to stick to."

"The way you've described things almost makes it sound like someone's messing with Nona," Aspen mused.

"If that were true it would certainly explain things. According to Nona, she woke and found Elvis #3 dead. She didn't touch him or look around; she simply freaked out and ran. The fact that the room was totally free of both a body and any blood less than ninety minutes later doesn't make sense. Especially because no one has reported seeing anything. But if Elvis wasn't really dead, if the knife and the blood were fake, I suppose I could see how he or whoever could have accomplished things in the amount of time allotted."

"The only real problem with that is why? Why would anyone go to all that trouble to play a prank on a harmless old lady?"

"I have no idea. And maybe that wasn't what happened at all. Maybe Elvis #3 isn't dead. Maybe nothing happened and Nona really is losing her mind. I guess all I can do is follow the clues wherever they lead."

"It doesn't seem you have a lot of clues to follow," Aspen pointed out.

"True. In this case I suppose I'll have to follow the lack of clues." I glanced at the clock. "Is there anything we need to discuss before I go?"

"Not really. When you arrived I was about to respond to a call about kittens in a drainpipe. The kittens have been living in and near the pipe with their mother, but the mother seems to have disappeared. The woman I spoke to is afraid she's come to some sort of harm, leaving the kittens on their own. She tried to reach them, but they were too far back in the pipe. We may need to trap them."

"Charlie and I will take a trap and some food and go over there on our way home. Do you have directions?"

Aspen handed me a paper with an address on it.

"I'm still going to come in tomorrow as scheduled. If things change, though, I'll let you know. Did you ever hear from the forest service about the bear cub they wanted to bring in?"

"The cub is being brought here in the morning. They said they'll arrive by around ten."

"Okay, good. I'll definitely be here then. This will be the first wild animal intake you'll be handling on your own."

"Okay. I'll lock up, so don't worry about that," Aspen assured me.

Charlie and I did a quick sweep of my office to ensure I wasn't leaving behind anything that needed to be dealt with, then we headed out of town to the address Aspen had given me. I hoped I'd find evidence that the mama cat was alive and well, but unfortunately, domestic animals left out on their own had to face a lot of hazards, including automobile encounters as well as run-ins with the large predators nearby.

The kittens had been spotted in a rural area. There were homes not far away, but they were widely spaced, so there was some forested area between each parcel of property. I loved living on the lake, but if I couldn't afford a home there, I'd want to live out in this unincorporated area rather than in town.

"Based on these notes, the kittens should be down in that drainage ditch," I said to Charlie as I pulled slowly to the side of the road.

If she was anywhere close by I didn't want the mama cat to be spooked by Charlie, so I left him in the car while I tried to suss out the situation. As Aspen had described, there was a small cabin just to the right of the ditch. I knew there was another property to the left, but the home wasn't visible through the trees. I walked slowly around, looking for any sign of the adult cat before I climbed down into the storm drain and took a look inside. I didn't see anything at first, so I took out my flashlight, then lay down flat on my stomach so I could get a look inside the pipe. I hadn't seen anything for a while, but then I saw something move. I'm pretty small, so while most adults wouldn't fit in the pipe, I was able to scoot forward until an orange kitten poked its head into view.

"Hey, sweetie. Is your mama around?"

I didn't see the mother and didn't want to risk leaving the kittens alone if she was gone, so I scooted back out the way I'd come and went back to the car for Charlie. It might seem counterintuitive to send a dog in after kittens, but I was afraid of crawling in any farther for fear of getting stuck, and the kittens were so young, I didn't think they'd be afraid of him. Besides, Charlie knew how to transport them without harming them, and he'd be able to travel farther into the pipe to ensure we didn't leave anyone behind.

"Find kittens," I said to Charlie after I'd prepared the crate for the kittens when he brought them out.

Charlie understood what I was asking and headed into the pipe. Less than a minute later, he came out with a white kitten that looked to be about three weeks old in his mouth. I transferred the kitten into the crate, then sent Charlie back in. Next, he brought out an orange kitten, then a black one, then another orange. I had him do one last sweep to make sure we had them all, then I set a trap for the mama just in case she came back. I'd swing by in the morning to check the trap. Hopefully, if she was still alive and nearby, I'd be able to capture her and reunite her with her babies.

When I was satisfied we had all the babies I loaded the crate into the car and Charlie and I headed home. I could take the kittens to the Zoo, but they were young enough to require bottle feeding for a couple of weeks at least, so I planned to take them home to Alex, who had fostered kittens in the past and knew exactly what to do.

"Ma," Catherine screeched when I walked in through the kitchen door.

"Kittens," Alex, who was sitting with Catherine, chimed in when she saw what I was carrying.

"They appear to be abandoned, although I set a trap for the mama just in case she comes back. I hoped you'd be willing to foster them."

"I'd love to." Alex grinned. "I'll set them up in my bedroom once I finish giving Catherine her snack."

I set down the crate with the four kittens near Alex's feet. "I can take over with Catherine," I said.

"Actually, you might want to go check in with Zak. The deputy who's taking over for Salinger came by earlier and spoke to both him and Nona. I wasn't included in the conversation, but I overheard enough to know the body of the man Nona swears to have seen this morning was found by some hikers this afternoon."

I let my smile slip. "So Nona was right. There *was* a murder."

"It sounds like it. Zak will know more about it. I'll finish up with Catherine, then put her down for a nap. Once she's settled I'll see to the kittens."

I gave Alex a hug. "Thanks, sweetie. I don't know what I'd do without you."

******

As it turned out, the man whose body was found in the woods wasn't Elvis #3. He was a transient who lived in the woods not far from where he was found. A deputy with any experience would have known right away that the man who was found wearing Elvis #3's blue sequined jacket wasn't the man to whom the jacket had belonged.

"So how does a transient end up wearing the bloodstained jacket Elvis #3 was wearing the last time I saw him?" Nona asked as she sipped on her before-dinner whiskey while she sat with Zak and me by the pool, enjoying the beautiful summer evening.

"I suppose someone, probably whoever removed Elvis #3's body from the motel room, could have disposed of the jacket, and the transient might have found it in a dumpster," I answered.

"Why would anyone want a jacket that was covered with blood?" Nona frowned.

"I don't know," I admitted. "Nothing about this makes sense."

"Do you think maybe the transient was in some way involved in Elvis #3's death?"

I glanced at Nona. "Maybe. It does seem the odds would be pretty astronomical that some random guy would find, take, and wear a bloodstained jacket he found in a dumpster, only to end up dead himself later that same day. Did the deputy say how the man died?"

"Buckner didn't have the medical examiner's report yet, but it appears the man died from natural causes, most likely a heart attack," Zak answered. "Like you suggested, he also suspects the jacket Elvis #3 was wearing when he was stabbed was discarded by whoever took the body and the transient found it in a dumpster."

"So he believes Nona's story?" I asked.

"I'm not sure he believes things went down exactly as Nona recalled them, but he's starting to come around to the idea that someone wearing the blue sequined jacket met with violence."

Nona picked up her empty glass and stood up. "I think I'm going to go in and lay down for a bit. I'm afraid all the excitement is beginning to take its toll."

"We're going to BBQ steaks in about an hour. Do you want me to call you when dinner's ready?"

"Just save me a plate. I think I might take a little nap."

"I hope she's going to be okay," I said to Zak after Nona went into the house.

"Me too. She likes us to believe she's a spring chicken capable of doing anything a woman half her age would be, but she really is getting on in years. I worry that her lifestyle is going to hurt her."

"Has she always drunk so much?"

Zak shook his head. "Before the stroke she was a teetotaler. I think the drinking, the motorcycle, and the devil-may-care attitude are all part of a persona I suspect was lurking beneath the surface all along. She seems a lot happier than she used to be, and I want her to be happy, but I'm just not sure how long her seventysomething body can keep up with her twentysomething lifestyle."

Zak wasn't wrong to be concerned. Nona did like to burn the candle at both ends. The problem with that was that eventually, the candle burned down completely.

"Did you ever talk to Levi about the weekend?" I asked him.

"I did. He said the entire Denton family would love to go sailing as long as the weather cooperates. I wasn't sure how sailing would mix with the morning sickness Ellie has been having, but he said she seems to be past the worst of it."

"I spoke to her yesterday and she said she was feeling a lot better," I confirmed. "She even seemed really enthusiastic about the baby for the first time since she found out she was pregnant again. We should check to make sure we have a life vest that will fit Eli. My mom and dad are going to watch Catherine for us, and we'll bring my little sister with us. We'll all meet back at the house for a BBQ after."

Zak stretched out his long legs. "Scooter mentioned he wanted to ask Tucker to come along. I told him it was okay."

"Just be sure to remind the boys that there'll be a toddler on board, so no horsing around," I reminded Zak.

"The kids know the rules."

Zak went in to grab the steaks for the grill, so I checked on the kids. Scooter, one of the two teenagers Zak and I were raising, was playing video games, and I reminded him that he'd need to wash up for dinner in thirty minutes. Alex was feeding the baby kittens, who seemed to have settled right in. After informing her that Zak had the steaks on the grill I headed to the nursery to check on Catherine. She was still asleep, so I began to speak to her softly. She hadn't slept all that long, but she needed to wake up now or she'd never sleep that night. Still, I'd learned long ago that waking her abruptly by picking her up usually left both of us in tears.

"Time to wake up, princess," I said softly as I walked around the room, straightening things. "Daddy's making dinner and we're going to eat out on the patio."

Catherine slowly opened her eyes. She looked around until she saw me, then smiled. "Ma."

I reached out my arms and she reached out for me. "That's my girl, all smiles for Mama."

I lay Catherine down on the changing table and took care of her wet diaper before grabbing a sweater against the chill I knew would follow the setting sun. I picked her up and carried her downstairs. I could hear the kids talking to Zak on the patio.

"Da."

"That's right. Da is grilling our dinner. Well, not your dinner," I amended as I walked out onto the patio, where Zak had already set up Catherine's high chair.

I sat her in her chair and gave her a small toy dolphin to play with, which made her giggle as if I'd just told the funniest joke she'd ever heard. I took out my phone to capture the moment with my camera. Not that I didn't already have a couple million photos of Catherine. She was, after all, the cutest baby in the entire world. After I snapped the photo I pulled it up to look at it. Displayed on the screen was the *Moments* view, which showed all the photos I'd taken that day, including the ones I'd taken from inside the motel room where Nona was sure Elvis had been killed.

"Zak," I said as my eye focused on one photo in particular.

"Yeah, babe?"

"Take a look at this." I pulled up the photo and handed my phone to Zak.

He looked at it and frowned. "When did you take this?"

"This morning. After we returned to the room I wanted to be sure I had photos of the place as we found it for future reference. But I didn't notice this until now."

"I guess we'd better call Deputy Buckner."

Chapter 5

Friday, July 6

"So, I'm taking photos of Catherine and I go to look at the result of what I'd taken and the photos I'd taken in Elvis's room earlier in the day are displayed on the same page," I said to Ellie the next morning as we shared coffee in my kitchen before I left for the Zoo and Ellie went to her mommy-and-me class. Both Eli and Catherine were sitting in high chairs next to us, cooing and chatting and having a grand old time. "Right there, plain as day, in one of the photos is an image of a man reflected in the bathroom mirror."

Ellie gasped. "Get out! You mean there someone in the room while you and Nona were looking around?"

"Apparently. I glanced into the bathroom when we first arrived, but the shower curtain was drawn and I didn't think to pull it open. I guess the guy must have pulled it aside and stepped out while I was snapping photos in the other room. I would never have seen him, but his image was reflected in the bathroom mirror, which was reflected in the mirror on the closet door."

Ellie tore off a corner of the blueberry muffin she'd been picking at for the past ten minutes. "I can't believe you were in the room for several minutes at least and had no idea there was someone watching you."

I nodded as I took a sip of my coffee. "Yeah, I was surprised by the photo as well, although I was taking the photos pretty quickly, and I was talking to Nona the entire time, so I wasn't paying a lot of attention to each shot. I was just trying to cover all the different angles. When I looked at the photos I could see I focused most of my attention on the bed and the floor near and under it. I must have thought if there was going to be a usable clue it would be near the murder site. I wasn't even trying to take a photo of the mirror on the closet door. I just caught it in the corner of the photo I took of the dresser."

"What did the deputy say when you showed him the photo?" Ellie asked as she handed Eli one of his toddler cookies.

"Zak was the one who spoke to him. I know Buckner had Zak send him copies of all the photos I took, and he sent a crime scene unit in to take a closer look at the room. I think he's finally beginning to get the idea that something very odd is going on."

"How's Nona doing with all this?" Ellie asked with a look of sympathy on her face.

I paused to consider. "She seems kind of overwhelmed, which I suppose is understandable. I can't imagine what it must have been like to wake up next to a guy who had obviously been murdered only to have there be no trace of him or the blood on the bed when she returned to the scene of the crime just ninety minutes later. There was one point when I saw a hint of doubt in her eye. It was while we were discussing the situation with Deputy Buckner. He made some good points about how things really couldn't have happened the way she described, and I think she might have been toying with the idea that she was losing her mind. The fact that Elvis's jacket was covered in blood when it was found seemed to add credence to her recollections, even though it's completely absurd that it was found on a different dead man."

"Have you heard anything more about that?" Ellie wondered.

I shook my head. "No, though Zak said the man has been identified. His name was Walton Welsh. It seems he'd been homeless for a number of years, but based on what Buckner was able to find out, he used to be a stockbroker. I guess he went over the deep end during the last big crash. He quit his job and left his family."

Ellie frowned. "How very sad."

"It is sad," I agreed. "I guess you never know when a single event will act as a catalyst to a complete breakdown."

"Did Bucker know why Welsh had the jacket?"

"He suspects he found it but wasn't certain. I guess he's going to ask around in the hope that someone might know more about what happened. Of course, now that he has the photo of the man in the room, I think he's going to be occupied with that."

Ellie looked once again at the photo of the reflection of the man in the bathroom. "The way this guy's head is turned you can't really see his face. Did Deputy Buckner think he could identify him?"

"No, it didn't sound like it based on what Zak said. Not with the photo alone. The forensic guys are working on it, and Buckner plans to take the photo over to the Elvis contest to show it to a few people. He hoped someone would recognize the guy based on his clothing, build, and hair color."

"Ma," Catherine screamed as loud as she could while throwing the piece of banana she'd been eating onto the floor.

I had to laugh at the ways she chose to get my attention. "What? Are we ignoring you?"

Catherine was looking at Eli.

"Are you mad that he has a cookie and you don't?" I handed her a baby spoon to play with, which she proceeded to bang on her high-chair tray.

Ellie used a wet wipe to clean up Eli after he finished most of his cookie. "I'm still amazed that Catherine can say *ma* and *da*. Eli wasn't talking at all until he was nine months old, and then it was hit and miss."

"Catherine is definitely Zak's child, at least in terms of her intelligence. I know she's only six months old, but I can already see how smart she is. She's really creative when it comes to communicating her wants and needs. She might not have words for everything yet, but I have a feeling she's going to be an early talker. Zak's mother told me he was talking practically from birth, which I'm sure was an exaggeration. She also said he was talking in complete sentences before he was a year old, which I totally believe."

"Catherine may have Zak's intelligence, but she looks exactly like you, with that dark curly hair and those huge blue eyes that already seem to mirror her emotions. If she ends up with your curiosity and spontaneity as well, I think you're going to have your hands full when she gets a little older."

"Let's just hope she ends up with Zak's easygoing nature. I'm not sure he'd survive if he had two emotional, spontaneous women on his hands."

Ellie smiled. "You do tend to attract more than your share of trouble."

"Tell me about it."

"Now that Buckner seems to have picked up the reins of the investigation, are you going to continue to be involved?"

My reaction was decisive. "I'm not. When I had Catherine, I promised Zak and myself I'd give up my sleuthing hobby. I wouldn't even have done what I did yesterday, except Nona was pretty frantic, and Buckner seemed to think she was just a crazy old woman who didn't know what she'd seen. Now that he's actively looking into things, I'm going to go about my day, starting with the Zoo. Do you and Levi want to come over for dinner? We can talk about our plans for sailing on Sunday."

"I'd love to come. I'll check with Levi and let you know what time works best for him, and I'll talk to Zak so we can coordinate the food. I'm happy to bring at least part of it. There's this new pasta salad recipe I've been wanting to try, and I've had a yearning to toss together a good old-fashioned potato salad."

I couldn't help but lick my lips. "My mouth is already watering. I think I'll invite my parents and Harper. She's going to come sailing with us while my parents watch Catherine for me."

"I'm surprised you aren't bringing her."

"Eli is all right in the water and able to swim with a life vest. If the worst happened and we had to abandon the boat, he'd be able to stay afloat. I haven't had a chance to spend much time in the pool with Catherine. I know the odds of anything happening are almost zero, but I'd still feel better if I knew she wouldn't panic if she did happen to end up in the water."

"I guess I don't blame you. When Levi wanted to start teaching Eli to swim before he could walk I thought he was nuts, but now he's pretty comfortable in the pool when Mom or Dad are with him. He hasn't spent a lot of time in the lake, but I'm sure by the end of the summer he'll be fine in the open water as well."

******

Later that morning, I worked side by side with Aspen as we got the cub settled into his temporary home. While most of the cubs we fostered were housed in a single large cage, we liked to quarantine new arrivals for a few days so we could check them out medically and evaluate their overall temperament. The cub was about three months old and had been orphaned when his mother had been hit by a car. He was shy, which wasn't unusual for a new arrival. If things went as planned, he would winter with us and then be released into the wild next summer.

"He's such a sweetie," Aspen said as she watched him eating the fruit she had just given him. "The only part of this job I'm struggling with is not getting too attached to every animal that comes through the door."

"It can be tough to keep your distance emotionally, which is why the Zimmerman clan has a house full of animals."

"How'd it go with the kittens yesterday?"

"I found four, but there was no sign of the mother. Alex is fostering them and I set a trap for the mother, but when I stopped by to check this morning I hadn't had any luck. I'll go back to recheck the trap later. If she's around I'd like to reunite mom and babies. If she isn't, Alex is off school for the summer and happy to take on surrogate mom duties."

"Alex is a great kid," Aspen commented. "Someday she'll make a wonderful mother after all the practice she's had with the animals she fosters."

"I'm not ready to even think about Alex growing up and having children, but I agree she'll be a wonderful mom someday. She's very nurturing." I handed Aspen our logbook. "Be sure to record everything you feed the cub into the log for the first few days. We want to keep an eye out for food sensitivities."

"Will do. By the way, how are things going with Nona?"

I took a few minutes to tell Aspen the news. When I spoke about the man in the photo she was as shocked as everyone else had been.

"You must have totally freaked out when you realized there was someone in the room with you the whole time," Aspen said.

"It was a bit of a shock."

"Do you think it was the killer?"

I narrowed my gaze as I considered Aspen's question. "It might have been, but it could have been someone else who'd broken in and was looking for something. I still haven't figured out how the killer got the body out of the room with no one noticing. The motel is booked. It was well into the daylight hours when Nona found Elvis dead on the bed. I've gone over it again and again in my mind, and no matter how I work things out, there just doesn't seem to be a reasonable explanation."

"What about interviewing the other eleven contestants? They're all staying at the same motel where that Elvis was murdered. Someone has to have seen something."

"I'm sure Deputy Buckner will interview the other Elvises."

"That doesn't mean they'll talk to him," Aspen pointed out. "Especially if they do know something and they're worried that it could either get them killed or get someone they know in trouble."

Aspen might be right. I really did want to let Buckner handle this, but not only was he a deputy, he was a green deputy. I'd promised Zak I wouldn't sleuth, but I didn't think anyone could find fault with me showing up at the competition and chatting up the other contestants a bit.

I helped Aspen clean the pens and dog runs, feed the animals, and process the current adoption applications, then decided to take a break and head over to the beach to see what was in store for the Elvises today. I knew they'd been introduced yesterday afternoon, and then there'd been a mini concert in which the contestants sang a song of their choice, but I wasn't sure where things went from there.

When I arrived at the beach the bandstand area was deserted. There was, however, a schedule posted on the wall. Tonight was the first elimination. Each Elvis would sing another song, then the judges would combine the scores from the two songs and eliminate the three Elvises with the lowest ones. I wondered if the fact that one Elvis had already left the competition would mean they'd only eliminate two Elvises tonight instead of three. I considered attending to find out, but I had guests coming for dinner, and I'd promised Zak I would stay out of things.

Turning over a new leaf was harder than I'd imagined it would be. It wasn't that I enjoyed putting myself in danger, but there was a part of me that found it extremely frustrating to be out of the loop, firmly planted on the sidelines.

"Excuse me, miss." A tall man with short dark hair, small eyes, and a pointy nose interrupted my pity party.

"Can I help you with something?" I asked.

"Are you associated with the competition?" he asked as he slowly looked me up and down in a manner I found to be uncomfortable.

I wasn't, but decided to fib to find out what was on his mind. "In a roundabout sort of way. Is there something you need?"

"I understand one of the Elvises has dropped out. I work for the costume company and hoped to collect the costumes Elvis #3 rented. We can rent them out to someone else if he won't be needing them."

"The Elvises rent their costumes? I figured they owned them."

"Some do, some don't. Each Elvis is required to have five different costumes for the competition. Even those who have costumes of their own don't necessarily have five."

"I'm surprised any costume shop would have so many Elvis costumes available in so many different sizes."

He shrugged nonchalantly. "We have a national presence. We brought costumes from all our locations to this event. So, about those costumes… Do you think I can grab them?"

I shook my head. "I'm sorry, I don't have access to the costumes. You'll have to wait for one of the administrative personnel to show up."

He frowned but didn't argue. I watched him walk away. Something felt off about this entire encounter. For one thing, I couldn't believe these Elvis impersonators rented their costumes. It seemed to me if you impersonated Elvis as either a career or a hobby, you'd have your own outfits. For another, I had to wonder why a costume company with a "national presence," as the man suggested this one had, would care about five costumes that most likely had been paid for for the entire event. Why would it be worth the effort to have someone come to collect them? If I had to guess there was, once again, more going on than met the eye.

Chapter 6

The man faded from view and I headed over to the board where the names and photos of the contestants were listed. I hoped if the man in my photo was another competitor I'd recognize him. I hadn't seen his face, but he was a man of average height and build with thick, dark hair that had been cut fairly short.

I eliminated each candidate based on those attributes alone. By the time I'd finished comparing the photos of the contestants to the one I'd taken, I was pretty sure he wasn't another of the contestants.

"Are you trying to choose a favorite?" asked a short woman with long red hair and rosy cheeks who both looked and smelled like strawberries who'd walking up beside me.

"I'm just trying to refresh my memory after the show last night. Do you have a favorite?" I asked politely, although I really didn't care.

"I've been following the competition from the beginning and I've settled on a few favorites. Ray here," she pointed to a man in the top row, third photo over, "seems to have the best stage presence, but he's a dud to talk to in person. In other words, the guy can sing, but he has zero personality. Personally, I think he'd be a terrible spokesperson over all."

"So. You've spoken to each of these men?"

The woman nodded. "I've made it a point to do so. In fact I know most of them quite well. Trent here," the woman indicated a man with blond hair, a friendly smile, and nice eyes, "is such a sweetie. He has all the personality you could want but a very weak voice. If I was going to choose a man to date out of all the Elvises I'd pick him hands down, but I think he'd bomb on the stage."

"What about him?" I pointed to Elvis #3.

"Calvin has the best costumes by far. Talk about bling. I should be so lucky to have even one dress as grand as his jackets."

"So he's extravagant?"

"In a sort of fun, sexy way. He has sparkly sequins and rhinestones on every costume in his wardrobe and I hear he has them custom made for each show he's involved in."

"Which means he wouldn't rent them?"

She looked scandalized. "Lord no. Any decent Elvis impersonator has a closet full of costumes to meet any occasion. They all have pretty wonderful stuff, but there was something really special about Calvin and the way he really brought the bling. I was sorry to hear he dropped out. I saw him in Vegas a couple of times and he was awesome."

"He'd performed before?'

"Sure. Lots of times. He was a pro until a couple of years ago, when he sort of disappeared. I heard he'd taken his impersonator gig on the road. I've only seen him impersonate Elvis, but I understand he has other acts as well. I heard he even had a gig in Europe for a while. I was thrilled to hear he was back in the United States, but then he goes and drops out just like that."

"With Calvin out of the running who's your choice?" I found I was curious now.

"Big Ben." She pointed to a broad-shouldered man with blond hair. "I know he doesn't look anything like the King, but once he's all made up he's passible. And his voice! Well, you know what I'm talking about if you caught the show last night. The man sings like an angel. And he's an all-around nice guy. He could use some work on his dance moves, but overall, I think he'd be the best bet. At least in my opinion. I guess everyone sees something slightly different in each of them. Or maybe they make us see something different. What they do, after all, is all about the illusion."

I supposed that at least was true. Everything that had happened in the past two days seemed like an illusion, if you asked me.

"I guess you're here for the weekend?" I asked.

She sighed. "I wish. I only stopped off on my way to my sister's. I'd put her off, but you know how it is with family."

"I do," I agreed.

After she walked away I headed back to my car, thinking about the possibility of everything being an illusion. Could everything that had happened since Elvis #3 had approached Nona in the bar been staged?

I couldn't imagine why, but at this point it was the only thing that made even a little bit of sense. On a whim, I took out my phone and called Deputy Buckner.

"Ms. Zimmerman, how can I help you?" he asked.

"The blue jacket Elvis #3 was wearing when he was killed, and Walton Welsh was wearing when his body was found. Do you have it?"

"I sent it to the crime lab. Why do you ask?"

"I have this feeling there's something odd going on with Elvis's costumes."

"Odd how?"

I explained about the man who'd claimed to be from the costume company, and the woman who was certain each Elvis had a closetful of costumes custom made for him. "I was curious whether the blue jacket was rented or owned. If it's rented it should have a tag from the company inside."

"Does it really matter?" the deputy asked.

"It might."

I listened as he let out a sigh. "Give me one good reason why knowing if the costume was rented or owned is important and I'll find out."

"If his costumes weren't rented it makes me wonder why the man I spoke to wanted them. Perhaps one of the costumes is the key. Maybe Elvis #3 had something sewn into the lining before he died."

I thought I heard him chuckle. "Well done. You managed to provide me with the one logical reason I asked for, so I'll have the jacket searched. I'll text you when I have something."

"Thanks." I smiled. "You're much nicer than Nona made it sound."

"Try driving a Harley down Main Street at double the speed limit and you'll find out how not nice I can be."

"Good to know. Before I hang up, do you have any other updates? I'll admit it's been hard for me to sit this one out."

"I can imagine," he drawled. "I called Sheriff Salinger and he filled me in on the Zoe Donovan-Zimmerman sleuthing team."

"The *retired* Zoe Donovan-Zimmerman sleuthing team," I countered. "I have a baby to take care of now. But still, with Nona involved, I'm finding I have the situation on my mind more than I ought to."

"I'm sure it's hard to change gears after all this time," he offered. "And while I have a few irons in the fire, I don't have anything I've been able to confirm yet. I might have news by the time I hear back about the jacket. I'll text you. And Zoe..."

"Yeah?"

"Salinger said he'd have my badge and my head if I let anything happen to you, so please, no sleuthing on your own."

"Don't worry. Like I've said, my sleuthing days are behind me."

When I'd been at the beach earlier I'd noticed the Elvises all planned to attend a cocktail mixer at Dirk Pendleton's home so his investors had the opportunity to meet the competitors. Or at least that was the supposed reason; having tagged along with Zak to similar events as a potential investor, this reception was probably more about Pendleton having the opportunity to raise additional funds. A few days in beautiful Ashton Falls was probably as much a motivator as many of Dirk's rich friends needed.

I wasn't an investor or a competitor, but I had the feeling if Zak asked Dirk he'd allow us to drop by and mingle with the group for an hour or so. We had the BBQ that evening, but Levi and Ellie weren't coming over until seven-thirty and the mixer was scheduled between four-thirty and six-thirty. The competition started at eight and the competitors had to check in at the beach at seven. I was sure Alex would be happy to watch Catherine while we were out, so I called Zak and ran the idea past him. I thought he'd just remind me that I was a retired sleuth and so had no reason to request an invite, but much to my surprise, he agreed the cocktail party was a good opportunity to chat casually with the eleven men who were the most likely to have some insight into what was going on. Once he confirmed we were good to go, I headed back to the Zoo to check in with Aspen, then went home to get ready for mixer.

******

Dirk Pendleton lived in a mansion right on the beach. The reception was being held on his huge deck, which I didn't think was quite as lovely as ours, though it had an excellent view and was only a short stroll down a paved walkway to the water. I'd worn a short dress with strappy heels that was appropriate yet left me yearning for shorts and flip-flops. Zak wore a dress shirt and pants, and we each nursed a flute of champagne.

"Let's split up," I suggested after we'd been greeted by Dirk, who took advantage of our presence to launch into his spiel about what a fantastic investment opportunity his casino was. Zak listened politely and asked all the right questions, but I doubted he'd end up investing.

"Okay. I'll start on the right side and you take the left. Be careful about what you ask. We want to find out what we can about Elvis #3, but we don't want to tip anyone off that it's our real purpose for being here. If Elvis was murdered it's very likely the killer could be one of the other impersonators."

"Don't worry. I'll keep it light and casual. Let's plan to meet in about forty-five minutes. We can compare notes and take it from there."

I went directly to the man the woman I'd spoken to earlier had identified as the nicest of the Elvises, Trent Pinedale, who was listed as Elvis #4. He had a nice smile and seemed happy and relaxed. I'd noticed some of the other competitors were all business, with a clear plan of action in mind to further their own popularity, but Trent appeared to actually be having a good time. Of course, all the competitors were drinking sparkling water rather than champagne, which made perfect sense because they had tonight's performance to consider.

"Trent Pinewood, I'm Zoe Zimmerman." I held out my hand in greeting.

"I'm happy to meet you. I saw you come in, but I didn't remember seeing your name on the guest list, so I wasn't able to put a name with the face."

I smiled. "Between you and me, my husband and I weren't on the guest list. We're almost what you'd call last-minute crashers."

Trent laughed. "Good for you. Gotta love a party crasher. I assume you live here in Ashton Falls?"

"We do."

"It's a beautiful place. All those green mountains cradling that beautiful blue lake. Do you work in the tourism industry?"

I shook my head. "Zak is a software developer and I own an animal rescue and rehabilitation center. How about you? Do you have a career other than being an Elvis?"

He took a sip of his water. "I'm a podiatrist."

I raised a brow. "A podiatrist?"

The man shrugged. "I like feet."

"How does it work, being a doctor and an Elvis impersonator? I can see being a bartender and an impersonator, or even a salesman and an impersonator, but a doctor?"

"Being a podiatrist is what I do for a living. Being an impersonator is what I do for fun. It's just like any other hobby. I plan my weekends and my vacations around the conventions and events I attend."

"But Dirk is looking for a full-time spokesperson. If you win do you plan to give up being a doctor?"

He chuckled in a deep, hearty manner. "If you're asking that question I'm going to assume you didn't attend last night's show."

I shrugged.

"I'm not going to win," he said. "I probably have the weakest voice in the competition. I'm just here for the fun it. The competition will wrap up on Sunday and I'll return to my real life on Monday."

I cocked my head to one side. "I like your attitude. I suppose that explains why you seem to be the most relaxed of all the competitors." I leaned in slightly. "Care to make a guess who'll win?"

Trent leaned in even closer. "Adam Weston, Elvis #12, is favored to win at this point. He has a strong voice, killer dance moves, and the most experience of any of the impersonators, with the possible exception of Calvin Jobs, Elvis #3. I know he's the favorite of both Dirk and the fans, but if I were a betting man, I'd put my money on Elvis #2. His name is Jason Michaels. He's a bit older than Adam and not quite as well known, but he has the look, the walk, and the talk of the real Elvis. If you have the chance to meet him, you'll see what I mean. When he's made up it's like talking to a ghost."

"I'll have to make a point of talking to him before I go." I took a sip of my champagne and tried for a totally nonchalant expression. "You mentioned Elvis #3, the one who dropped out, had the most experience of anyone, yet when I spoke to Dirk yesterday he said he thought he dropped out of the competition because he got cold feet."

Trent laughed. "There's no way Calvin had cold feet. The guy is a pro and has been doing this sort of thing for a long time. He even did some stuff overseas. In fact, over the past two years he's been going back and forth between Europe and the United States quite a bit. I think there might have been a woman involved in his sudden fascination with foreign gigs, but I don't know that for certain. What I do know is that he definitely didn't go into insurance after quitting Vegas like everyone says."

"It would be fun and interesting to be able to travel as part of your job, no matter what the reason."

Trent shrugged. "I suppose. I think the travel took a toll on Calvin, though. Or maybe it was the woman he was seeing that took the toll. The last couple of times I ran into him, he looked tired, and it looked like he'd lost some weight. I think maybe he got in over his head with all the running around. When I saw he'd entered this competition I hoped it meant he was done with all that and ready to settle into a permanent situation again."

I noticed Dirk had waved at Trent out of the corner of my eye.

"It looks like duty calls. It was nice meeting you."

"You too," I answered. "And good luck, even if you are just in this for fun."

I managed to interview three additional Elvises before Zak motioned that it was time to go. We said our good-byes to Dirk and then headed for the truck.

"So, what did you think?" I asked.

"In a nutshell," Zak began, "it appears Calvin was a popular guy, although everyone I spoke to said he'd been really stressed lately. I heard more than once that he'd been spending quite a bit of time overseas the past couple of years, but he might be back in the States permanently now. On the last night anyone saw him he seemed to be in a good mood and having a good time. No one I spoke to had any idea why he'd dropped out of the competition. I did talk to one Elvis who said Calvin received a call earlier that day. He wasn't sure who he'd been speaking to, but he seemed to be refusing to do whatever he was being asked to do."

"Dirk said he'd overheard Calvin on the phone talking about the stress being too much and not being able to follow through. Dirk thought he meant the competition was causing him the stress, but no one else had that opinion. What if there was something else going on? What if he got mixed up in something bad? Something he might have originally agreed to but then changed his mind about. What if the something he didn't feel he could follow through with is what got him killed?"

Chapter 7

Later that evening I held Catherine in my arms while we walked around the pool. Ellie had placed Eli in an infant ring that allowed him to kick his legs and splash the water with his hands while remaining safely afloat. I'd eventually try Catherine out in the ring when she got used to me holding her in the water. Zak had the temperature of the pool adjusted so it was like floating in the bathtub.

"Remember, no diving off the side or splashing around while the babies are in the water," I reminded Scooter, who had just come running out from the house with his best friend, Tucker.

"We'll be careful." Scooter held up a fist full of colorful hard rubber rings. "We're going to dive down for the rings in the deep end, but we won't splash at all."

"Okay," I said. "That sounds fine. Where's Alex? I thought she was playing video games with you."

"She's on the phone with Diego. She was whispering, so me and Tucker couldn't hear what she said, but I think she was talking all lovey-dovey to him." Scooter made a face that conveyed his disgust. While Alex and Scooter were the same age, she was a lot more mature in almost every way, including her feelings about the opposite sex. While Scooter was in many ways a late bloomer, I had the feeling it wouldn't be long before he was involved in intimate telephone conversations with his own crush of the moment.

"Da." Catherine reached out a hand for Zak as he joined us in the pool.

"How's my girl?" Zak asked as I shifted Catherine from my arms into his. I didn't want to be jealous that Catherine was most definitely a daddy's girl, but there was no denying that if we were both in the room she preferred that Daddy be the one to hold her, or rock her, or give her a bottle. "Are you having fun with Mommy?"

Catherine slapped the water, sending drops into my face as a response.

"I'd really like to teach her to swim this summer. Eli is already paddling around between Ellie and Levi, and he isn't afraid in the least to float around in his ring."

"Do you remember Dalton Rivers?" Zak asked.

"The guy who had you build a totally new security system for his company?"

Zak nodded. "Anyway, when I was in Los Angeles installing the system he invited me to his house for dinner. His son was about Catherine's age then, and he was already swimming. He wasn't walking yet, but once he was in the water he paddled around like a little puppy. He's four now, and he can do laps in an Olympic-size pool. Who knows, he might be an Olympic contender someday."

"I don't care about the competition thing as much as making sure Catherine is comfortable in the water and knows how to swim. Owning a pool and living right on the lake, the skill is crucial."

"I agree." Zak laughed as Catherine grabbed his nose and let out a squeal.

Levi had entered the pool to supervise Eli and Ellie got out. I left Catherine with Zak and joined her. She looked tired today and I was concerned she might be overdoing. She seemed to be doing fine with her surprise pregnancy now that she was finally getting used to the idea, but I remembered those first months of my own pregnancy, when all I wanted to do was sleep.

"Eli is really doing a good job in the water," I said as I dried my hair. "He's going to be swimming across the pool by the end of the summer."

"Yeah." Ellie smiled. "He's got his daddy's athletic ability. Levi got him this little plastic bat and he's trying to teach him how to hit the little plastic ball it came with, and he can already throw a mini football."

"He's only fifteen months old."

Ellie shrugged. "He's doing pretty good, actually. He can swing the bat now; Levi just has to teach him to watch for the ball. I thought I'd head in and start getting the sides together so they'll be ready when the guys grill the meat."

"I'll help," I offered. "I just want to run upstairs to put on some dry clothes."

After changing out of my swimsuit into a pair of denim shorts and a baby blue tank top, I braided my hair, then headed downstairs to the suite where Nona was staying. Deputy Buckner had told her to stay home and keep a low profile until he figured out what was going on. Nona had agreed to do so, a promise I was certain she'd never keep, but so far, she'd barely left her room, let alone the house. I had to admit her willingness to stay out of things had me more than a little concerned.

"Nona," I called as I knocked on her door. "It's Zoe. Is it okay if I come in?"

I waited for several seconds before Nona, dressed in a bathrobe, opened the door.

"We're going to be having dinner in a little while. Zak is BBQing if you want to come down," I encouraged.

"Thanks, but I think I'll just make a sandwich and eat it in my room."

"Are you feeling okay?" I asked. "You usually love Zak's chicken and ribs, and Ellie made baked beans and several salads. It's a lovely evening and I thought we'd eat out on the deck and watch the sun set over the lake."

"It sounds nice, but there's a *Golden Girls* marathon on. I think I'll just stay here."

I raised a brow. "You hate *The Golden Girls*. You once told me that an entire TV show about a bunch of old women was ridiculous."

Nona lifted a shoulder. "I changed my mind. They aren't so old. Younger than me. And they do get themselves into some comical situations. You go ahead and have a nice evening with your children and your friends. The last thing you need is some silly old woman hanging around."

I hugged Nona. "You may be silly sometimes, but you aren't old. At least not old at heart. If you change your mind come on down. If not, I'll bring you a sandwich before we eat."

"Thank you, dear. My Zak found himself an angel when he found you."

An angel? That didn't sound like Nona at all.

When I entered the kitchen, Ellie was stirring the potato salad. "What's with the scowl?" she asked.

"I popped my head in to check on Nona. She's not going to join us for dinner because there's a *Golden Girls* marathon on television."

Ellie gave me a skeptical look. "Nona hates *The Golden Girls*."

"I know. I asked her if she felt okay and she said she was fine, but I have my doubts."

"I guess she might just be dealing with the stress of Elvis #3's death. I know she'd just met him, but still… I can't imagine what must have gone through her mind when she woke up and found him lying there."

I opened a drawer and took out a knife. "Yeah, I guess it could just be that, but I feel like there's more going on. She might be a bit under the weather despite her assurances to the contrary. It would be just like her not to want to worry me, but the *Golden Girls* thing is just too weird."

"Nona is getting on in years. Maybe she's starting to see the humor in the process instead of fighting the inevitable tooth and nail."

"Maybe. But if her mood change results in her giving up everything that makes her so unique, I'm going to find it very sad."

"Wasn't it you who tried to get her to give up the bike and drive something safer and more age appropriate?"

I sighed. "It was, but now I'm sorry I said anything. She went from being a crazy but vibrant risk-taker to being a faded shadow of the woman I knew and loved in just twenty-four hours. If she isn't back to her old self by tomorrow I'm going to see if she's willing to get a checkup."

Ellie placed her hand on mine as I cut tomatoes like a wild woman. "Nona has had a tough couple of days. Give her some space and some time. I'm sure she'll be back to driving you crazy in no time."

"I hope so."

"Can you grab the paprika?" Ellie asked as she stirred the potato salad.

I handed her the spice, then used a spoon to take a bite. "That's so good. It's been a while since you made it."

"I usually only make it to serve with summertime BBQs and I haven't felt up to making something so labor intensive until recently."

"Is the morning sickness gone?" I asked sympathetically.

"Mostly. Every now and then I still feel queasy when I first wake up. At least Levi has been home to help with Eli now that school's out."

"Is he still talking about getting a job for the summer?" Levi had made some noise about earning extra money during his time off.

"No. We talked about it and he understands I need the help at home right now. Besides, once football practice starts up in a few weeks he'll only have a few hours a day free anyway. And given that our very best friends in the entire world allow us to live rent-free in their fabulous boathouse, we're actually doing pretty well financially even without any income from me."

I smiled. "You know Zak and I are happy to have you and Levi in the boathouse. It gives us peace of mind to know we don't have to worry about renting it to some random person who might not take care of it as if it were their own the way you and Levi do. And with the remodel there's room for all the Dentons."

"I'm excited to decorate the nursery before the baby's born. Not that I didn't appreciate you allowing us to live here while the boathouse was being remodeled, but the timing eliminated the need to really prepare for Eli at least in terms of getting his room ready."

I took a watermelon out of the refrigerator and began to slice it. "I don't blame you a bit. You'll have fun with the planning once you know if you're having a boy or a girl."

"I'm excited about finding out, although I'm torn about which I want. Part of me really wants a girl because I've always dreamed of having a little girl of my own, but a second boy might be better so Eli would have someone to roughhouse with."

"Girls can roughhouse," I reminded Ellie. "I certainly did."

"True. But there's no guarantee a boy and a girl will get along."

"There's no guarantee two boys would get along either," I said.

"I guess you have a point. I know the baby's gender is one of those things that's already decided and out of my hands, so I'm trying not to overthink it."

I picked up the pitcher of ice tea and headed to the back door. "Not overthinking it is a very good idea."

******

After the Dentons left I went to check in with Nona again. When I'd taken her a sandwich she'd instructed me to leave it on the table. I wouldn't be at all surprised to find she hadn't eaten it. I hoped she was simply fighting off a cold and there wasn't something more serious going on.

"Nona." I knocked on the door. "It's Zoe. Can I come in?"

She didn't answer one way or the other, so I quietly opened the door and slipped inside. The television was still on, but Nona was nowhere in the room. I glanced in through the open door of the bathroom, but she wasn't in there either. "Nona?"

When it was obvious the suite was deserted, I went back downstairs to have a look around. She wasn't in any of the rooms, so I headed out onto the front drive. "Oh, Nona. What are you doing?" I said to myself when I saw her Harley was missing. Turning around, I went in search of Zak.

"Nona's missing," I told him.

"Missing?"

"She wasn't in her room when I went to see her, so I checked the drive. Her Harley is gone."

Zak's lips tightened. "If she wanted to go out why wouldn't she just tell us?"

"Because Deputy Buckner told her to stay close to home and she was probably afraid if she told us she was going out we'd try to stop her. She didn't want to argue, so she pretended to be enthralled with a *Golden Girls* marathon. We've been around back all evening. She could have left at any point."

"I'll call her," Zak offered. "Maybe she'll answer her cell."

She didn't.

"Should we go look for her?" I asked.

"You stay here with the kids and keep trying to get her by phone. I'll take a run by her favorite bars. Hopefully, it won't be a problem tracking her down. If she comes home or answers a call text me."

"You might want to find out where the Elvises are tonight. I have a feeling Nona might be out doing a little sleuthing of her own."

Zak looked at his watch. "What time did the competition end?"

"Everyone had to have a chance to perform and the first three Elvises had to be eliminated. I guess you should check the beach first. Even if the contest is over there might be stragglers."

"Okay. I'll call you after I check out the beach. If you think of anything else call me."

"If she isn't at the beach check the motel where the Elvises are staying. If she is trying to figure out what happened to her the other night, she might go back there to talk to whoever's around."

"Did she mention any of the other Elvises by name?" Zak asked.

"No. She pretty much referred to them by number. She mentioned one who dressed all in white. I think she said he was Elvis #7. And I spoke to Trent

Pinedale at the party today. He seemed really nice and isn't in the competition to win. He'd probably tell you what he knows if he knows anything."

It didn't take Zak long to find Nona's pink Harley parked in the beach parking lot where the competition had been held. The only problem was, the contest was over, the crowd was gone, and there was no sign of Nona anywhere.

Chapter 8

Saturday, July 7

When Deputy Buckner called the next morning to let us know that Nona had been released from jail and had been sitting in front of the sheriff's office for the past hour, I was outraged. First, I demanded to know why Nona had been arrested.

"Drunk and disorderly conduct."

Okay, I hated to admit it, but that fit.

When I asked why we weren't called immediately, he said he'd allowed Nona to call us and, in fact, had sat across the desk from her while she did so. She spoke to Zak, or at least pretended to speak to Zak, then reported that we'd already gone to bed and weren't able to come to get her.

Apparently, she'd lied.

Her Harley had been impounded because overnight parking at the beach, which she must have circled back around to, was illegal. We were informed that we'd need to pay the impound fee to get it out. Deputy Buckner said he'd offered to give her a ride home, but she'd refused. He'd assumed she had a ride lined up, but considering she'd been sitting on the bench in front of his office for over an hour, he was beginning to doubt that was true. This, it turned out, was why he'd called me when he had.

"Keep an eye on her and make sure she doesn't leave. I'm on my way," I assured the temporary deputy.

"Was that Nona?" Zak asked when I passed him on the stairs.

"Yeah. She needs a ride. I'm going to grab my purse and pick her up."

Zak frowned. "Where's her bike?"

"In impound. It's a long story. I'll fill you in when I get home."

"I can go," Zak said.

I shook my head. "No, it might be better if I go. I won't be long. Catherine is in her jumpy chair in the den with Alex and Scooter. All three are watching cartoons."

When I arrived at the sheriff's office and saw Nona sitting like a forlorn child on the bench in front I wanted to cry. I carefully pulled into a parking space and sat for just a moment as I tried to decide how to approach the increasingly unpredictable woman. Deciding to play it by ear once I got a feel for her mood, I got out and walked across the lawn.

"Beautiful day," I said as I sat down next to her.

"Humph."

"It looks like you could use a ride."

"I have a ride. I just need some money to get it out of motorcycle jail."

I took Nona's hand in mine. "Do you want to talk about it?"

"Nothing to talk about. I went out, had a good time, and ended up in the slammer. It happens. Now, about the bike…"

"I'll take you over to the impound lot to get it. But once we do, you and I and Zak are going to sit down to talk about whatever it is that's causing you so much distress."

"I'm fine," Nona grumbled.

"No. You're not. I'm worried about you. Zak is worried about you. We love you and want you to be okay."

"I'm not a child. I don't need to be coddled."

I closed my eyes and counted to ten. "You're not a child, but every now and then we all need to be coddled. Zak and I love you. Let us help you."

Nona bent her head but didn't respond. I had the feeling she might be crying, but I knew overreacting wouldn't be the best move, so I just waited. Eventually, she sat up straight, looking into the distance but seemingly resigned to my request.

"Are you ready?" I asked.

Nona nodded.

"Okay. Let's go get your Harley. After that I want you to go straight home. Take a shower. Get something to eat. Zak made muffins for breakfast. I think there are some left. I need to run to the Zoo for a couple of hours, but when I get home we're going to sit down and figure this out."

"They still haven't found his body, you know."

"Elvis #3's?" I asked.

Nona nodded. "The Elvises had an after-party down the beach from the event location. I decided to tag along to see if I could pick up any clues about what might have happened to him. Most of the other Elvises think he just changed his mind about the competition and took off. They think I either imagined the dead body in the bed or am making it up. They made it pretty clear they think I'm just some old woman who's lost her mind. They want me to stop talking about it. They think a murder would be bad publicity for the contest. They want me to go about my business like it never happened."

"What about the jacket with the blood on it?" I asked. "That seems to prove you didn't make the whole thing up."

"Not human."

I frowned. "What do you mean, not human?"

"The deputy told me the blood on the blue sequin jacket wasn't human. The crime scene guys are doing some additional tests, but they think it's cow blood. The other Elvises think I got it from a butcher, poured it on the jacket, then tossed the jacket somewhere it would be found. They think this whole thing is a ploy to get attention. One of the Elvises went on and on about his own grandmother, who's about as loony as they come, but at least she never tried to fake a murder."

"Okay, wait. You said you were passed out and when you came to, Elvis was dead. You said he was lying on the bed next to you with a knife in his chest. You said he was lying in a pool of blood. Did he have his jacket on?"

Nona's eyebrows furrowed. She twisted her lips and looked up toward her forehead. "I'm not sure. It was all kind of a blur. I was in shock. I wasn't thinking. I just saw him and left. I went to get you and you know the rest."

"What if the whole thing was staged? What if Elvis wasn't actually dead? What if he only wanted to make you think he was?"

"Why on earth would he go to so much trouble?"

"I have no idea."

******

The concept that Elvis had faked his own death began to take hold now that I knew the blood on his jacket wasn't human. We still had no way of knowing if the blood on the bed was real, but Nona had said that she woke up, was disoriented, saw Elvis lying in a pool of blood with a knife in his chest, then fled. She hadn't touched him or felt for a pulse. What if he had been faking, then cleaned everything up and took off as soon as Nona left the room?

Of course, that theory was about as crazy as any was likely to be, but it had planted itself in my mind and I decided to take a day to really think about it. I'd told Aspen I'd be in to the Zoo for a while this morning so we could take care of any last-minute adoptions. Brothers Tank and Gunnar were taking over the care of the animals from the time the Zoo closed at noon on Saturday until nine o'clock on Monday morning, when it reopened for business, so unless there was an emergency of some sort I should have a day and a half with no work obligations.

"We have three pickups this morning," Aspen informed me. "All have been vetted. The files are on your desk if you'd like to take a look at them before they arrive. I also got a call about a dog neighbors say has been chained to a tree for the past three days. I can run over there to take a look if you want."

"Thanks, Aspen, but it might be better if you handle the adoptions while I respond to the animal cruelty call. Most of the folks in the area know who I am and are familiar with my link to animal rescue, while you're still pretty new to the Zoo and the community. What's the address?"

Aspen rattled it off.

I frowned. "That's Mr. Trout's house. I hope he's okay. It's not like him to leave his dog out for any length of time. I'd better go now. Call me if you have any questions when the new pet parents show up."

Barney Trout had lived in Ashton Falls at least as long as I had. He used to work at the post office but had retired. He owned his own home, where he lived with his Lab, Gus. Gus was friendly, like his owner, and loved to socialize, which meant Barney and Gus could be seen around town, talking to folks they met along the way, on most days of the week.

The only problem with Gus was that he was a wanderer. This trait in and of itself might not have proven to be a challenge except that a portion of Barney's fence had blown over a few years back, so Barney had taken to chaining Gus in the yard for short periods every day. It wasn't like Barney to leave Gus in the yard for three days straight, however. I really hoped both dog and human were all right.

The first thing I did when I arrived was check on Gus. It looked like his bowl had a self-watering feature attached to the sprinkler system, but there was no way to tell the last time he'd been fed. I went to the house and knocked on the door. "Barney? It's me,

Zoe Zimmerman. Are you home?" When there was no answer I knocked again. After several more knocks I tried the knob. It was unlocked.

"Barney," I called as I entered the house. Still no answer. "Are you home? It's Zoe." When there was still no answer I began searching the house room by room. I put a hand to my mouth when I found Barney lying on the floor of his bedroom. I hurried over to his side and felt for a pulse. He had one, but barely. I took out my phone and called 911.

I looked around the room as I waited for the ambulance. There was a box of tissues plus a whole lot of over-the-counter medications. If I had to guess I'd say Barney had contracted the flu. Unfortunately, it appeared it had gotten the upper hand. Once the paramedics arrived and had transported Barney to the hospital, I went for Gus, who I decided to take home rather than to the Zoo. The poor guy was pretty shook up and he'd do better in a house with a family to take care of him.

"Are we getting a new dog?" Scooter asked the minute I walked in with Gus.

"No. This is Gus. We'll just be taking care of him while his owner is in the hospital. I'd like you to take charge of walking and feeding him."

"You want me to foster him like Alex is fostering the kittens?" Scooter beamed.

"Exactly. Can you do that?"

Scooter nodded. "Come on, Gus. I'll introduce you to Charlie, Digger, and Bella," Scooter said, and took him off to meet our three family dogs.

"Are you home from the Zoo already?" Alex joined me in the kitchen.

"No, I need to go back. Did Nona make it home okay?"

"Yes, and she went up to her room. Zak's putting Catherine down for a nap and I was about to log on to the computer."

"I really should get back to the Zoo. Tell Zak I'll be home in a couple of hours."

Alex took an apple from the bowl and took a large bite. "Zoe, is Nona okay? She didn't look very good when she got home."

"She had a rough night. I don't have all the details, but I thought Zak and I would sit her down and have a talk with her when I get home. In the meantime, if you need anything call or text me on my cell."

By the time I returned to the Zoo, Aspen had completed all the adoptions and was in the process of creating some notes for Tank and Gunner to refer to over the weekend. Between the two of us we'd been handling things just fine, but I'd still be glad when Jeremy got back from paternity leave and Tiffany got back from her honeymoon.

"How was Mr. Trout?" Aspen asked.

I filled her in.

"I hope he's going to be okay. Poor guy. It's tough when you live alone and are sick or injured. There's no one to help you out."

"Yeah." I couldn't help but think of Nona. She was staying with us for a few months, but during most of the year she lived alone. Maybe I'd talk to Zak about asking her to move in with us permanently.

"We had an intake while you were out," Aspen said. "Border collie who looks to be a year or two old. I've quarantined her until the veterinarian who's filling in for Scott can look at her, but she appears to be healthy and well fed. She was picked up by a motorist on the highway. In my opinion she's probably lost. I'm going to upload her photo to all the usual sites. If her owners are located I'll have Tank or Gunnar call me. I'll come down to take care of the paperwork so we can get her back to her people right away."

"Thanks, Aspen. I do hate it when pets are separated from their family. Other than helping Nona figure out exactly what's going on with her Elvis dilemma, I'm around the rest of the afternoon. I'm planning to go sailing tomorrow, so I may not be reachable even by cell, although if you need me for anything you can leave a message and I'll return it when I find a hot spot."

"I'm sure everything will be fine. Have fun on the water. It's supposed to be warm and sunny all weekend. I heard we might even be looking at highs in the mid-eighties."

"I did hear there was going to be a warming trend. I'll try to check in when I can."

Aspen waved me off. "Go. Enjoy your weekend. I'll make sure things run smoothly here. You have nothing to worry about. I promise."

Chapter 9

As soon as I got home I checked on all three kids and then went to find Zak. It was going to be important for us to present a united front when we spoke to Nona. She'd always been a handful, but she'd been even more unpredictable than usual the past few days.

"Are you busy?" I asked Zak when I found him in the computer room working on a project.

"Not really. Catherine was napping and the other two were occupied, so I decided to work on the new security software Zimmerman Industries hopes to unveil in the fall. Are you finished at the Zoo?"

I nodded. "I'm home for the rest of the weekend. Is Nona still in her room?"

"I think she may be napping. I guess spending the night in jail isn't all that restful. I understand why Deputy Buckner took her in, but I can't believe she didn't call us to come get her."

"She might have been embarrassed, and I got the feeling she didn't want to be a bother to us. I'm really worried about her."

Zak sighed. "Yeah, me too."

"I think the first thing we need to do is help her figure out what's really going on with Elvis #3. I know we agreed to retire from sleuthing now that we have Catherine to think about, but I'm afraid Nona isn't going to let this go until she figures out what really happened, and I don't want her out there digging around on her own. I figure if we put our heads together we can solve this increasingly confusing puzzle."

"I agree," Zak said. "In fact, I've already done some digging that I hope will provide us with a starting point."

I sat down on a chair next to Zak. "Great. What do you have?"

He pulled up a screen that displayed the notes he'd assembled while I'd been at the Zoo. Calvin Jobs, aka Elvis #3, was forty-seven years old. He'd worked as an Elvis impersonator at one of the Las Vegas casinos for five years prior to quitting two years before. Over the course of the past two years, he'd traveled extensively. His most recent trip was to Monaco, where he was hired for a four-week stint to do impersonations for a cabaret show in one of the casinos. Before that he'd worked in other clubs and casinos in Italy and France.

"Someone I spoke to mentioned that while Calvin seemed to have been working overseas the past two years, he flew back and forth between Europe and the United States on a regular basis."

"That's correct. In fact, I was able to find evidence that he made transatlantic flights twelve times in the two-year period."

"That's a lot of flying."

"It seems as if it would have made more sense for him to stay in Europe for longer periods, rather than do so much hopping back and forth, but there may have been a reason for his frequent returns to the States. Perhaps there was a woman involved. Someone he came back to spend time with every couple of months."

"Okay, so we know Calvin flew back and forth between Europe and the United States a lot. What else do we know?"

"Based on what I could find in my initial search, his finances were in a bit of a mess. It appears he spent more traveling back and forth across the ocean than he made with his short-term jobs. Unless he has money stashed somewhere I haven't found yet, the guy was flat broke."

"It seems crazy to travel so much if he couldn't afford it. I feel like the traveling is a clue. It's an anomaly that doesn't make sense. Did he have money prior to quitting his job in Vegas?"

"Not really," Zak said. "Based on some of the money transfers I've been able to identify, I'm going to go out on a limb and say Calvin had a gambling problem. I'd also be willing to bet the reason he left the country in the first place had something to do with a gambling debt."

"You think he was running away from someone? Maybe someone he owed money to?"

Zak shrugged. "Maybe. Or maybe he went to Europe to complete some sort of a task that would help him pay off his debt."

"A task?"

"Smuggling comes to mind. Or perhaps it had to do with access to the casinos where he had these jobs. I can't be sure, but it makes sense to follow the money and see where it leads."

"Except he didn't have any," I pointed out.

"He didn't have any that I've been able to find. Yet. I'll keep looking."

I sat back and considered the situation. I wasn't sure if figuring out what Calvin had been up to in the months and weeks prior to his encounter with Nona would help us understand whether he was dead and if he was, who'd killed him, but it couldn't hurt to have all the pieces of that puzzle. "I think you may be on to something with the smuggling idea. When I was at the beach the other day a man approached me, saying he was from the costume company who rented Calvin his costumes and wanting to collect them because he no longer needed them. I later learned Calvin had his own costumes that he had custom designed and made. What if he was using the jackets to smuggle something back and forth across the ocean? What if the man who approached me knew that and was looking for the costumes not for their value in and of themselves but for something hidden in the pockets or sewn in the lining?"

"Something in a pocket or sewn into a lining would still come up in a scan," Zak pointed out.

I hesitated. "Maybe. Still, I think the costumes are going to turn out to be an important clue. When Calvin came back to the States did he have a home base to return to? Maybe an apartment he kept even though he was away so often?"

"Not that I've been able to find. It appears he stayed in cheap motels when he was in the States. When he was overseas his accommodation was often provided by the casinos he worked for."

"It doesn't make sense that he would have carted all his stuff back and forth. He must have had a storage shed at the very least."

Zak leaned back in his chair, crossing his arms over his chest. "You make an interesting point. I'll look for something like that. Although he could have kept his stuff in a friend's garage for all we know. Still, looking for a storage shed makes sense."

I got up and began to walk around the room. I often found that pacing helped clear my mind, especially when I was filled with pent-up anxiety. "What it really comes down to is that one of three things is most likely true: Calvin is dead and someone really killed him, in which case we need to find and help apprehend the killer; or Calvin isn't dead, and for reasons unbeknownst to us he staged his death and took off, which would mean we need to find him so we can prove it and move on; or Nona really is losing her mind and imagined the whole thing."

"I thought you believed me."

I cringed, turned, and saw Nona standing in the doorway. Talk about lousy timing. "I do believe you. Zak and I were just talking about all the options. Are you feeling better?"

"Depends. Are you going to help me find Elvis's killer?"

"We are," I answered decisively. "Zak has already started working on it. Come on in and we'll catch you up."

Nona had a scowl on her face, but she came all the way into the room and took a chair. "I'm not crazy."

"I know. I'm sorry. Zak and I suspect Calvin might have staged his own death."

"Why would he do that?" Nona asked.

"Maybe he was in some sort of trouble and needed to disappear," Zak suggested.

"So why involve me?" Nona asked. "Why the elaborate illusion?"

"If Calvin wanted to fake his own death he'd need a witness," I said. "It sort of makes sense in a sick, twisted way. He brings you to his room and drugs you so you pass out. Then he sets up the murder scene with a fake knife and fake blood. Once you see he's dead you leave, at which time he cleans everything up and takes off for wherever he planned to hide out."

Nona crossed her arms and looked at me. "What if I hadn't left? What if I stayed right there and called 911? What if I waited in the room until help arrived? That is, if you think about it, what any normal person would do."

Nona was right. There was no way Calvin could have counted on the variable of Nona leaving the scene, Darn. It seemed we were back to a real murder and a real killer to find.

"I think we need to operate under the assumption that Calvin really was murdered," Zak said. "While there's a possibility Calvin had a reason to want to fake his death, things become much too complicated once you start to think through the entire situation."

"So if he's dead where's his body?" Nona asked. "And what's up with the animal blood on the blue sequined jacket? I can't remember whether Elvis was wearing it when I found him dead on the bed, but I do know he was wearing a blue sequined jacket that evening."

I looked at Zak. "What should we do?"

"Talk to the other Elvises," Zak answered.

"That'll only get you tossed in jail," Nona warned.

"I'm not going to get drunk and pick a fistfight with someone who's equally drunk. Zoe and I will go over to the competition and work the crowd. Hopefully, someone will know something that will help us make sense of things."

"Talk to a woman named Vera," Nona suggested.

"Who's Vera?" I asked.

"She's a sometime girlfriend of Elvis #3. I met her last night. She's young. Pretty. Seems like she could do better than a worn-out Elvis impersonator, but I think she's genuinely concerned that Elvis left the competition. She mentioned to the others that she'd been trying to contact him, but he wasn't answering his texts or calls. She also mentioned a friend she planned to contact: Gavin. I don't have a last name or any other information, but if you can find Vera, she might be willing to give you what you need."

"Okay," Zak said. "Anything else?"

"Elvis #2, Jason, seemed to be the most vocal about the fact that Calvin had gotten in too deep, like he tended to do, and had taken off as a result. He didn't specify what it was he was too deep in to, but the others seemed to agree. Like I told Zoe earlier, the consensus was that Calvin was alive and well and I'm just some crazy old woman who's making the whole thing up."

"Jason is the one Elvis #4, Trent Pinedale the podiatrist, felt was most likely to win the competition. I suppose if Calvin was a strong contender, which it seems he was, having him out of the way will only help the guy."

"Okay," Zak said. "We'll make a point to speak to Jason and Vera. Anyone else come to mind?"

"Yolanda. She's some sort of Elvis groupie. She didn't seem to be attached to any one Elvis, but she shows up at a lot of events where the Elvises appear. I didn't much care for her attitude and might have said some rude things to her about her overall appearance, so you might not want to mention the connection between us."

"Does Yolanda have a last name?" I asked.

"I'm sure she does, but I don't know it. Ask around. She's tall and thin with big red hair. She has a Brooklyn accent that fades in and out depending on the amount of alcohol she's consumed. She speaks loudly and has a lot to say about everything. She was with the Elvises at the bar the night I met Elvis #3. I think she could know something, but the two of us took a dislike to each other right away, so she wasn't in the right frame of mind to share when I started asking questions. You know," Nona tapped her chin, "on that first night I met Elvis #3, after we all went to the beach, not only was Yolanda there but she had a friend with her too. I can't remember her name—I'm not sure I ever knew it—but someone might be able to tell you."

"Okay. That gives us a starting point," Zak said.

"I'll call my mom to see if she can watch Catherine for a couple of hours," I said. "I don't want to ask Alex to give up her Saturday babysitting."

"I can watch her," Nona offered.

I looked at Zak with a plea on my face. I didn't want to make Nona mad by indicating that I didn't trust her with my baby, but I didn't want to leave Catherine with her given her current state of mind.

"Actually, Ellie called earlier to say she was planning to pick Catherine up. There's some sort of event being sponsored by the mother's group she belongs to and she wanted to take both babies," Zak said.

I let out a sigh of relief. "I'll call her to let her know we're going out. We can just drop Catherine off on our way to the beach."

Chapter 10

Tall and thin with big red hair. As it turned out, big red hair was an understatement. Yolanda Green sported a bright red beehive that would have made her grandmother proud. Not only was Yolanda dressed as some sort of tribute to the sixties, but she seemed to have embraced the free-love lifestyle I personally witnessed as she engaged in a lip-lock with one Elvis after another.

"Yolanda?" Zak had finally been able to catch her between men and stepped up to introduce himself.

"Well. hello there, handsome." Yolanda licked her bright red lips. "Are you alone?"

"He's with me," I said as I hurried forward to stand next to my husband before this very aggressive woman got her claws into him.

Yolanda raised a brow. "I see." She turned her attention back to Zak. I couldn't help noticing the way she leaned forward to expose her ample bosom. "What can I do for you?"

Zak smiled in a manner I found much too flirty, but I was sure it was just a tool to help loosen Yolanda up so she would tell us whatever she knew. From the way she was throwing herself at Zak, and the way I'd seen her throwing herself at every other man within a ten-mile radius, I was pretty sure she was in on the intimate details relating to the personal lives of quite a few of the Elvises.

"I understand you're a regular at this sort of competition," Zak began, "and know many of the Elvis contestants personally?"

Yolanda ran a long red nail up Zak's arm, paused, then ran it down again. I wanted to slap her but refrained from doing so.

"I do have a bit of an Elvis fetish," Yolanda replied. "I don't suppose you'd want to borrow a costume and go for a test drive?"

Hello. I'm standing right here!

"Actually," Zak answered, after sending me a warning glance, "I was hoping you knew something about Calvin Jobs—Elvis #3—and his disappearance from the contest."

Yolanda raised a brow. "You a friend of his?"

Zak lifted a shoulder. "A friend of a friend. Do you know anything?"

Licking her lips, Yolanda replied, "I might. Buy me a drink?"

Zak glanced at me. I nodded. Yolanda grabbed him by the arm and dragged him toward the tent that had been set up to sell alcohol and other cold beverages. I figured Zak would be at least fifteen minutes, so I decided to look around to see if I could find Elvis #2. The Elvises all seemed to be loitering in the area, mingling with judges and spectators. Elvis

#2, Jason Michaels, supposedly was the most convincing of them all when in full costume. Based on what I'd heard, it appeared the contest would most likely have come down to Calvin Jobs and Jason Michaels. With Calvin out of the way, Jason was at a huge advantage.

"Excuse me," I said to a woman who wore an ID tag indicating she worked with the competition. "Can you tell me which contestant is Elvis #2? I believe his name is Jason Michaels."

She pointed to a man holding court near the bandstand. "That's Jason. He has rehearsal in fifteen minutes, so if you want to speak to him, you'd best hurry."

"Okay. Thank you." I turned and walked quickly to where Jason was speaking to a group of people, both men and women. I honestly was shocked at the amount of attention this competition was getting. There was live television coverage from a crew out of Bryton Lake of the actual competitions and a film crew was on hand to shoot material for a future television feature.

"Mr. Michaels," I interrupted the conversation he'd been having. I hated to be rude, but getting the guy alone wasn't going to happen if I played by the rules of etiquette. "My name is Zoe. I wonder if I could speak to you for a moment about a private matter."

"A private matter?"

"Involving Calvin Jobs."

Elvis #2 turned back to the group and said, "Sorry for the interruption. If you'll excuse me I'll find out what's on this young lady's mind, then come back in this direction."

The group seemed fine with the arrangement, so I walked a few steps away from them and I jumped right in with my first question. "I know you're on a tight schedule, so I'll be quick. I'm related to Nona. I assume you know who I'm referring to?"

"The crazy dame with the pink hog."

"Yes. I imagine you've also heard she believes she witnessed Calvin Jobs's murder. Well, she slept through the actual murder, but she witnessed the result."

"So she says. Personally, I don't buy it. Calvin had some problems. Quite a few, from what I've heard. He was fired from his job in Vegas, and instead of doing what any normal guy would do and get a job in another casino there, he upped and went to Europe. I don't have all the details, but it seems Calvin got hooked up with some guy who was in to some illegal activities that can not only get you arrested but can get you dead. Last I heard, he had some guy on his tail and was getting nervous. Chances are the heat was getting worse, so he took off."

"Do you know who Calvin was in business with or who might have been after him?"

"Talk to Leroy Jenner: Elvis #1. He was good friends with Calvin at one time. If anyone knows what was really going on it most likely was him."

"Do you think there's any possibility whoever was after Calvin caught up with him and killed him?"

Michaels shrugged. "Sure. But if whoever was after Calvin killed him, the dame with the pink bike would be dead too. Guys like that don't leave witnesses. Even unconscious ones."

He was probably right. If Calvin had been killed by a professional thug there was no way Nona would be alive to witness what she was sure she had.

By the time I'd finished speaking with Elvis #2, Zak was making his way back to the spot where he'd left me.

"Sorry about that." He kissed me on the forehead. "The last thing I wanted was to have a drink with her, but I did want to find out what she knew."

"And did she know anything?" I asked.

"Yes, she did. Let's find a place to sit away from the crowd and I'll catch you up."

I followed Zak to the little trail that led from the sand bordering the lake to the parking area that served the entire beach. About halfway up the trail we found a bench in the shade and sat down.

"According to Yolanda, Calvin got hooked up with a man named Darwin Monceaux, who deals in precious gems. Illegally obtained gems, to be more precise. Yolanda wasn't sure exactly how Calvin fit into the whole business, but basically, Monceaux and his team steal jewelry in one country, remove the gems from the settings, and smuggle them into another country, where they're sold on the black market. While Monceaux has never been caught or prosecuted, it's widely known among Interpol agents and other jewel thieves that the man behind the theft and smuggling ring is very well protected."

"So maybe Calvin was a courier." Suddenly it hit me. "The costumes. Calvin didn't smuggle anything into or out of the country in the pockets or lining; he smuggled the gems by replacing the rhinestones on his jackets with the real thing."

"Makes sense. I'm assuming Calvin was messed up or simply wanted out and Monceaux either killed him or had him killed."

"The problem with that is," I pointed out, "if a professional criminal like Monceaux killed Calvin, he would never have left Nona alive."

Zak frowned. "That's a good point. Even though she was passed out cold, a professional wouldn't have taken the risk."

I sat back and stared off toward the crowd that was beginning to gather. "Elvis #2 said Calvin had been in some sort of danger before his death. What if Monceaux or his employees were leaning on Calvin? Maybe he'd messed up, or, as you suggested, he simply wanted out of the game. When I spoke to Dirk the other day he said he overheard Calvin on the phone. He didn't hear everything, but Calvin said the stress was too much for him and couldn't follow through with his commitment. Dirk took that to mean his commitment to the competition, but he might very well have been referring to the smuggling operation."

"I imagine that wouldn't have gone over well."

I leaned forward and rested my elbows on my thighs. "The kind of activity Calvin seemed to have been involved in isn't the sort you can just walk away from because it no longer suits you. I can understand why he might have wanted to disappear. Earlier, we discussed the idea that Calvin faked his death. I'm beginning to think that's a better theory then I imagined initially. The only hiccup is the part Nona brought up, about the unpredictability of her leaving the scene, giving Calvin the time he needed to clean up and run. Most people *wouldn't* have taken off the way she did. Most people, me included, would have called 911 and waited until help arrived, which would mean Calvin wouldn't have had the opportunity to make his getaway."

"Unless he accounted for the possibility that Nona would stay and had a plan B in place," Zak pointed out.

"What sort of a plan B?"

Zak leaned back and crossed one long, darkly tanned leg over the other. I could see his mind was working through a scenario. "The Elvises are professional impersonators. Many of them impersonate a number of different people. They're good at what they do and, more importantly, they're believable. What if someone was helping Calvin? Maybe someone was hiding and watching from a connecting room. If Nona hadn't left, if she had stopped to call 911, maybe there was a plan for Calvin's accomplice to intervene."

"Maybe the accomplice was dressed like a cop or an EMT?" I was beginning to catch on. "If Nona made the call, or tried to, this other person would have shown up and sent her on her way."

"It's a theory. Maybe not a completely developed theory, but a theory."

I stood up and began to pace in front of the bench. "How do we prove this? How do we prove any of it?"

"We find the accomplice."

I paused and snapped my fingers. "Leroy Jenner. Michaels said Elvis #1, Leroy Jenner, was friends with Calvin. If our theory is correct maybe he's the accomplice we're looking for."

Zak looked at his watch. "The next round of rehearsals are about to start. Let's grab a beer and a seat and watch. We can track down Leroy after they're finished. If we time it right we can grab Leroy just as the contestants are leaving the stage."

"Okay, but let's be sure not to miss him. It might be hard to find him after everyone goes their separate ways." I took Zak's hand and we headed toward the beer tent. "Did you think to ask Yolanda about the friend Nona referred to?"

"I did. Her name is Priscilla. Or at least that's what she goes by. According to Yolanda, if she's around you can't miss her. She has dark hair and dresses to look like a young Priscilla Presley."

"How would a young Priscilla have dressed?"

"Pretty much like anyone else from that era, but if she's intentionally trying to impersonate her it should be obvious." Zak looked around the tent. "Pretty much like that woman sitting at that table over there."

"Good catch. What do you say we wait on the beer and sit down next to Priscilla before someone else does?"

As it turned out, Priscilla was a very nice woman who seemed to be in to the whole role-playing thing but otherwise was fairly normal.

"Sure, I know Calvin. He's been part of the business for a long time. Nice guy. I was sorry to hear he'd dropped out of the competition."

"Do you have any idea why he did?" Zak asked.

Priscilla shrugged. "I don't know for sure. I do know things changed for Calvin after he was fired from his gig in Vegas. He moved around a lot and stopped showing up at the various events and competitions. Most people felt he was embarrassed about being fired, but I think there might have been more to it. If you ask me, there was a woman involved in at least part of what went down, although I don't know exactly how it all comes together."

"Do you have any idea who the woman might have been?"

"Not for sure. He never mentioned a name or anything. I did see him outside a convention center once a couple of years ago talking to a woman. I thought he was pleading with her about something, but she ignored him, got into a cab, and left. I swear, it looked like he was crying. I didn't want to intrude on such a personal moment, so I slipped back inside without saying anything. Two weeks later he was fired from his job for showing up to work drunk. I can't say for certain the two things were related, but the timing suggests as much."

"Do you know anything about Calvin's life outside his role as Elvis?" I asked.

"Not really. I've never heard him mention a significant other or children. He did talk about a sister once in passing. I'm not sure they had much of a relationship. Calvin was a nice-enough guy, but he seemed sort of reckless to me. I heard he fell in with some bad people. I wasn't surprised."

"Do you know what he was up to after he was fired from his job in Vegas?" I asked.

Priscilla shrugged. "Like I said, I heard he fell in with some bad people. I know he was out of the country for a while. I'm not even sure when he came back. Before this week I hadn't seen him in more than two years. In fact, the scene with the woman was the last time I saw him until he showed up here."

"Did you notice anything unusual or significant about him or his behavior when you saw him earlier this week?"

"It looked as if he'd lost weight, but he really needed to. He seemed to be having fun with the others. I guess he seemed somewhat distracted but not unusually so. It was weird that he hooked up with that old broad. She had to have been a good thirty years older than him. Calvin was a popular guy. He could have gotten someone a lot younger to keep his bed warm."

"So he didn't normally prefer more mature women?" Zak asked.

Priscilla laughed. "Not Calvin. He usually went for twenty-year-olds. No, the old dame was strange. I'm not sure what that was all about. The only thing I've been able to come up with is that the old dame was helping him with some sort of a prank."

A prank. Now that was a simple solution I realized deserved a bit more attention.

Chapter 11

Leroy Jenner was a short man with a slightly plump body who didn't look all that much like Elvis, though when Zak and I caught his rehearsal while we were waiting to speak to him, he had a strong voice and adequate moves. Afterward, Zak pulled him aside to ask if we could speak to him. He seemed amenable enough, but I got the distinct impression from our first question to the last that he was either holding something back or downright lying.

"What did you think of Leroy?" I asked Zak as we drove back to the house.

"He knows something. I don't know what it is, but it seemed obvious his answers were guarded. When we asked if he thought it was possible Calvin had faked his own death either as a prank or as a means of escaping a bad situation, I could see his muscles tighten and his face turn red."

I rolled down my window and let the warm air caress my cheeks. "So, are we going with the faked death hypothesis?"

Zak bit his bottom lip. "Maybe. At least for now. Without a body or real blood or anything concrete, we don't have any proof that he's actually dead. And if Leroy, or someone, helped him, things become even more plausible."

"We need to get Leroy to talk," I said. "I don't think Nona is going to let this go unless we turn up proof one way or another."

"I agree. We'll need to come up with a plan."

"I was thinking we'd give him a bunch of money in exchange for his telling us what he knows." There was nothing better than keeping it simple.

"That might work, but if Calvin is in trouble and Leroy really is his friend, he may not rat him out even for financial gain."

"Yeah. I guess that's true. Don't forget, we need to pick up Catherine at Levi and Ellie's."

"I'd never forget to pick up my Catie Cue."

"Catie Cue?"

Zak grinned. "It's a new nickname I'm trying out. You didn't like Little Pooter."

I laughed. "You need to be careful with nicknames. Sometimes they stick well into adulthood."

"You mean like Stinky Jeffries?"

"Exactly like Stinky Jeffries." We were thinking of a kid we went to school with. He'd been given the nickname Stinky by his older sister and that's what everyone still called him in high school.

Levi and Ellie were on the back deck overlooking the lake with both babies sitting quietly in their strollers between them. Levi was sipping on beer and Ellie had a bottle of water. Zak and I were offered our choice and both went with water.

"Beautiful evening," I said, after I'd greeted my baby and taken a seat next to Ellie, who had her feet propped up on the side of the fire pit.

"It is beautiful, and very relaxing, until we begin discussing baby names," Ellie agreed.

"I thought you didn't know the baby's sex yet," I said.

"We don't and won't for another month, but we decided to pick both a boy's and a girl's name. So far, the only thing we've been able to agree on is that we don't care for the other person's suggestions."

"Not that I want to get in the middle of this, because I don't, but what do you have so far?" I asked.

"Jerry if it's a boy and Jeri if it's a girl," Levi said without even taking a beat to stop and think about it.

"Jerry?" I raised a brow.

Levi raised a brow. "After Jerry Rice, the greatest wide receiver of all time."

"I don't want my child named after a football player," Ellie argued.

"Eli is named after a football player," Levi said.

"No," Ellie said firmly. "He isn't. He's named after us. *El* from the first two letters of my first name and *i* from the last letter of your first name. The fact that there happens to be a football player named Eli is strictly a coincidence."

I seemed to remember having this same conversation when Ellie was pregnant with Eli. Levi had wanted to name his son after a football player that time around as well. I turned and looked at Ellie. "What names would you choose?"

"I have a long list already, and my top choice has changed several times. Right now, I like Julia if it's a girl and Ramsey if it's a boy."

I rolled my eyes. "Really? The fact that you want to name your child after a famous chef is just as ridiculous as Levi wanting to name the baby after a football player."

"Julia is a common name. Naming my daughter Julia won't mean I'm naming her after Julia Child. And naming our son Ramsey doesn't necessarily mean I'd be naming him after Gordon Ramsey."

Zak sent me a stern look that left me in no doubt that he'd prefer I not get into an argument between either of my best friends.

"You're right. I'm sorry," I apologized. "I really don't want to be in the middle of this. Julia, Jerry, and Ramsey are all good names."

Ellie sat back and let out a groan. "No, they aren't. I mean, of course they're fine names, but they aren't fine names for us. We picked them for all the wrong reasons."

"How about Jordan for either a boy or a girl?" Levi suggested.

Ellie paused. "Football?"

"Nope," Levi assured her with a self-satisfied grin.

"Basketball," I supplied. "I do like the name for either a boy or a girl, though."

"Maybe we need our own family ghost," Ellie said. "You settled on Catherine so easily."

Ellie had a point. I knew if I ever had a girl I was going to name her Catherine long before I became pregnant. Of course, having a psychic tell you that you're descended from a strong, independent woman who became a strong, independent ghost living in a haunted Irish castle is apt to make a lasting impression.

"I didn't choose the name because of my discovery of Catherine the ghost. I chose the name because Catherine was my ancestor. It has meaning to me. What about family names?"

Ellie frowned and Levi did too. It seemed they were at least considering this approach.

"I think we should get this little pumpkin home," Zak said before standing and picking up Catherine, who looked thrilled, as usual, to be in Daddy's arms.

"Are we still on for sailing tomorrow?" Levi asked.

Zak and I both hesitated.

"Would Monday work for you as an alternative?" Zak asked.

Levi and Ellie indicated it would.

"It's just that we haven't figured out this Elvis thing yet, and tomorrow may be our last day to work on it," I explained. "Once the contest winner is announced tomorrow evening I'm sure the Elvises will scatter, and we'll have no way to find our answers. I'm afraid wrapping this up has been hard on Nona."

"Of course getting the answers Nona needs should take priority," Levi said. "Can we help? Maybe we can watch Catherine again?"

"That might be best," I said. "Can I call you after we speak to Nona?"

When we got home Alex was in the kitchen making spaghetti. The sauce was simmering on the stove, a pot filled with water to boil the noodles stood ready to be turned on, and two loaves of sourdough bread were buttered and ready to be stuck into the oven. My stomach started to rumble even as my heart filled with appreciation.

"Where's Scooter and Nona?" I asked as Zak handed Catherine to me, then washed his hands before pitching in and assembling the ingredients for a salad.

"They're playing video games. They've been in there since you left. Did you find the person Nona was looking for?"

"Not yet," I answered. "But I feel like we're starting to put things together."

"I hope you can figure it out. Nona's still really upset," Alex said. "I've never seen her so depressed. It's starting to scare me."

"The degree to which this is affecting Nona is scaring me as well," I agreed. "I almost wonder if something else is going on. Did she say anything to you?"

Alex shook her head. "No, though she seems to have this bipolar thing going on. One minute she's chomping at the bit to get out there and solve the mystery on her own, the next minute she's sulky and quiet. She goes from being angry about everyone referring to her as an old woman to referring to herself as an old woman. I do think there's more going on than just the stress of the dead or missing Elvis. You should probably take her to see a doctor."

"I had that same thought. I'll make an appointment for her next week. In the meantime, we're postponing sailing until Monday and working on the Elvis mystery tomorrow."

Alex grabbed a large spoon and stirred the pot of sauce. "Scooter will be disappointed, but I think that's a good idea. And I want to help. I went online and pulled up the list of contestants, then did a basic search of each of them. I found a few interesting things, although nothing that really indicates what might be going on. Still, I thought we could go over what I found after dinner."

Zak shot out an arm and hugged Alex to his side in a gesture of silent approval. From the huge grin on her face, the gesture meant a lot to her.

Dinner was as delicious as it had smelled. Afterward, I headed upstairs to bathe Catherine and put her down for the night while Zak did the dishes, Nona went to her room to rest, Scooter went into the den to watch TV, and Alex returned to the computer room to continue with her search. Zak and I planned to meet her there to see what she'd found once we'd completed our evening tasks.

"Maybe we can keep the splashing to a minimum," I said to Catherine as I set her into a baby tub filled with warm water that Zak had set into the larger tub, which helped to catch the water spilled over by baby hands and feet.

"Ma," Catherine screeched as she slapped the water, hitting me squarely in the face.

"Did you have fun playing with Eli today?"

Catherine laughed and splashed me again. This was apparently hysterical; she laughed again and splashed even harder. My heart filled with love as I watched her antics. She was such a sweet, agreeable baby. She was hardly ever fussy, and if she was, you knew something was definitely wrong.

Catherine looked a lot like the photographs I'd seen of myself as a baby: rosy cheeks, bright blue eyes, curly brown hair that fanned her face like a halo. I wondered if she'd be petite like me or tall like Zak. So far, she'd been weighing in at just about dead center for a baby her age.

I tossed a rubber duckie into the water, which delighted Catherine even more. These end-of-day rituals were important to both of us, and I tried never to miss them unless it absolutely couldn't be avoided. After she'd splashed most of the water out of her little tub, I wrapped her in a large, fluffy towel, then talked to her playfully as I dried her off. Once she was dressed in a warm, fuzzy onesie, I warmed her bottle and settled into the comfy chair in front of the gas fireplace. I clicked the fire on, lowered the lights, and hummed a lullaby as Catherine had her final meal of the day. When she was done, I tucked her into her crib, turned on the baby monitor, and headed down to the computer room to see what Alex and Zak were up to.

"Catherine all tucked in?" Zak asked as I walked in.

"Sleeping like a little princess. So, how's it going down here?"

"Alex did an excellent job of digging up something on each of the contestants, including Calvin," Zak informed me. "She clearly has your sleuthing instincts and my computer know-how."

I smiled and Alex grinned from ear to ear. There were a lot of thirteen-year-olds who wouldn't want to have anything to do with their parents, but I knew Alex was grateful for our giving her a real home, something she'd never had with her biological parents. She sought and appreciated praise and recognition from both of us, but especially from Zak, who was not only a father figure but a mentor and role model.

"Were you able to narrow things down?" I asked. "We only have one more day before everyone scatters. If there's someone who knows the truth about this crazy mystery we need to focus in and get the information we need."

"Alex and I have been talking things through. At this point it's our theory that Calvin got into trouble with the wrong people and faked his own death to simply disappear. Based on what we've ascertained, it seems Calvin targeted Nona specifically, maybe because she was a senior and he figured the sheriff's office would be more apt to take her seriously, or maybe because she looked to be vulnerable. We suspect his plan all along was to be seen partying with her that evening, so there would be witnesses that could corroborate Nona's story that she'd spent time with him on the night he 'died.' After they'd been seen by the other contestants, Calvin took her to his room and drugged her. She fell into a deep sleep, during which time Calvin set up his illusion, probably with someone else's help. As we've realized, the only way his plan could work is if Calvin had someone standing by to intervene should Nona have called 911 rather than leaving his room, as she did. We suspect Calvin's accomplice might be Leroy Jenner, Elvis #1, because they were friends. I was able to pull Calvin's phone records, and he did speak to Leroy late on the evening of his supposed death, though that doesn't prove anything except that they were in contact. Because we're assuming that Calvin's accomplice may have been keeping an eye on him from an adjoining room, I pulled the motel records and found that Elvis #7, Connor Brown, was staying in the room on the other side of room fourteen's connecting door."

"Elvis #7 is the one who was always dressed in white," I said. "He's the one who invited Calvin and Nona to the party on the beach. If everything was staged, as we suspect, he could very well be Calvin's accomplice."

"Alex and I agree," Zak said. "We pulled his banking records. Calvin transferred twenty thousand dollars into Brown's account the day before he supposedly was murdered."

I frowned. "I thought you said Calvin was broke."

"I did say that. And it appeared to be true after my first sweep of Calvin's finances. But Alex dug deeper and found an offshore account. The money he transferred to Brown came from that account."

"So how do we prove this?" I wondered.

"I think it's time to get Deputy Buckner involved. Connor Brown may have accepted twenty thousand dollars from Calvin in exchange for helping him fake his own death, but I'm pretty sure he won't be willing to go to prison for him. All Buckner has to do is charge him with Calvin's murder and my guess is he'll be more than willing to give us the proof we need that Calvin is alive and well."

Chapter 12

Sunday, July 8

"Zak," I screamed as I ran down the hallway. It was two o'clock in the morning and I'd gotten up to check on Catherine when I'd heard a noise. When I arrived at her room I saw she was sound asleep, but that was when I realized the noise I'd heard was really from Nona's room. I knocked twice. When she didn't answer, I let myself in.

"Catherine?" Zak asked as he stumbled groggily out of our suite into the hallway.

"Nona. I heard a noise and went to check on her. She's on the floor, unconscious."

"Call 911," Zak said as he started down the hallway.

I'd left my cell on my bedside table, so I went back to grab it and make the call. It only took the paramedics fifteen minutes to respond, but when a person you care about is unresponsive, fifteen minutes seems like an eternity.

"I could see something was off earlier," I said as I stood next to Zak, praying everything was going to be okay. "She's been so withdrawn the past few days."

"We still don't know why she passed out," Zak, who was kneeling on the floor, monitoring her heartbeat while we waited, reminded me.

"I should have checked on her earlier."

Zak took my hand in his. "It's not too late. Nona is unconscious but alive and her heartbeat feels steady. The paramedics will be here in a few minutes. It's going to be okay."

I really, really hoped so. I didn't know what I'd do if Nona died.

Zak accompanied her in the ambulance, and I followed behind in my car after waking Alex and letting her know she was in charge of Catherine should she wake. Alex was naturally upset about the situation, but I knew I could count on her to keep a level head and do whatever needed to be done until we returned. To be honest, I was the Zimmerman who was having the most difficult time keeping it together.

"How is she?" I asked Zak when I arrived. He was sitting on an uncomfortable-looking couch in the waiting room.

"I don't know. They wouldn't let me follow her in and the doctor hasn't come out yet. She was alive but still unresponsive when they wheeled her in."

My instinct was to curl up into a ball and sob, but I needed to try to be strong for Zak, even though that was the last thing I was feeling. I reminded myself that while I'd only known Nona a few years, Zak had known her his entire life. Nona wasn't actually his grandmother, wasn't, in fact, related to him by blood. She was the mother of his cousin Eric's father. Eric's mother was the younger sister of Zak's mother.

"Should we call someone?" I asked. "Your mom? Eric? Wanda?"

"No," Zak said decisively. "Eric's family cut Nona out of their life after her stroke. They don't feel it's dignified for a woman her age to be carrying on the way she does. Personally, I find Nona to be a lot more human and enjoyable since her stroke caused that drastic personality change."

I squeezed his hand. While it was true Nona started out life controlled by rules and etiquette, since I've known her, I'd found her to be not only strong and opinionated but just a tiny bit crazy. "You know how I feel about her. I love her just the way she is."

"Mr. Zimmerman." A doctor wearing a white jacket entered the waiting room.

He rose. "Yes, I'm Zak Zimmerman."

"I'm Dr. Whitmore, filling in for Dr. Westlake."

"Where's Dr. Westlake?" I asked.

"He is doing a stint with Doctors Without Borders."

Now that he mentioned it, I seemed to remember our usual doctor telling me his plans a while back. Charlie was a therapy dog and we used to stop by the hospital all the time, but my life had gotten so busy the past couple of years, I'm afraid offering comfort to hospital patients had been one of the things I'd pushed onto the back burner.

"How's Nona? Is she going to be okay?" Zak asked.

"She's stable at the moment. Your grandmother is suffering from the effects of a tumor that's putting pressure on her brain."

"Is it dangerous?" I asked.

"There's risk involved with any surgery, but I think there's real hope for a full recovery."

"Real hope? What does that mean?" Zak asked.

"I'd say the odds of her doing just fine is better than fifty percent."

My heart sank. Fifty percent.

"Your grandmother has already had at least one stroke, and we found evidence of minor heart attacks as well," the doctor continued. "I suspect her blood pressure has been high for quite some time. It seems to have gone untreated. Does your grandmother drink?"

Zak nodded. "A lot."

"One of the scans we did showed liver disease. These medical issues, along with her age, will unfortunately add to the overall risk of the surgery."

Zak bowed his head. "I understand. When do you want to operate?"

The doctor hesitated. "There's a neurosurgeon in the hospital in Bryton Lake. He'd be a better choice than anyone here."

"Make the transfer," Zak said. "I'm going to follow the life flight helicopter down."

"I'll follow you with the truck. I'll call Ellie and ask her to either come stay at our house or pick up the kids and take them to her place." I hugged Zak. "Nona's a fighter. She's going to pull through this."

"I really hope so."

******

The next few hours were some of the tensest of my life, but after waiting while the neurosurgeon at Bryton Lake did his own assessment, and then pacing the halls of the waiting area of the surgery center for almost seven hours after he decided emergency surgery was in order, he finally came out and told us Nona was stable and in recovery. Zak wanted to see her, but he was told she was still out from the anesthesia and would be for quite some time, so we'd need to come back the following day. We thanked the surgeon and headed out to Zak's truck.

"I'm exhausted," I said as we pulled out of the parking lot. "I spoke to Deputy Buckner. He's having Connor Brown brought in for questioning when the competition is over. He said we could watch the interview through the glass if we wanted to." I glanced at Zak. "I'd like to. If you aren't too tired."

"I'd like to as well. When Nona wakes up I really want to be able to tell her that we have the whole story and she can stop worrying."

"If Brown isn't being picked up until after the competition, we should have time to stop by the house. We can take showers and change into clean clothes. We'd probably feel better if we ate something too. I'll call Ellie to let her know what's going on." I paused, then added, "Don't you think it might be time to call your mother to let her know what's going on?"

Zak sighed. "Yeah. I guess. I'll do it as soon as we have a chance to regroup. I'm not sure I can deal with whatever snarky comment she's likely to make."

"It's too bad your mom and Nona don't get along. I'm sure that makes things hard on you."

Zak didn't respond, but I could see by the look on his face that he agreed.

"I guess if you think about it, we're the only family Nona has who she has a relationship with."

"While it's true most of the family wants nothing to do with her, the rift between them is mostly her fault. Still, I feel bad about the way things are. Nona has a lot to offer if the others would just give her a chance."

I chuckled. "I understand not everyone can take Nona's brand of crazy. Still, I adore her, and I worry about her. Even before this, I was thinking maybe we should talk about having her move in with us. We have the room now that Pi has moved out," I said, mentioning our third almost-child, "and she's going to need help, definitely in the short term but possibly forever."

"She'll resist the idea," Zak said.

"She will, but we can be forceful when we need to be. She can't keep living her life the way she has." I paused. "I take that back. She can keep living that way if she doesn't care about being around for years to come. We both know her lifestyle is a recipe for a disaster of some sort."

Zak wiped his eyes with his fingers. The poor guy looked exhausted. "Okay. When she's awake and alert and completely out of danger, we'll talk with her. The doctors are going to insist she has care for the short term at any rate. We can work on a long-term arrangement from there."

"I really think once she gets settled in she'll be happy. She adores you and she adores Catherine. She's a big fan of Scooter's video games and seems to enjoy chatting with Alex. On her own she might have excitement and her freedom, but with us she has a family."

By the time we got home it felt like we'd been away a week, not just a bit more than thirteen hours. I made us something to eat while Zak showered and changed. I figured it was most important for him to have a clear mind because he would be the one driving. I'd decided to heat up the leftover spaghetti from the night before by repurposing it into a spaghetti casserole. It actually looked and smelled wonderful. Zak still wasn't down by the time I slipped the casserole into the oven, so I called Ellie.

"How's Nona?" Ellie asked.

"Alive."

"I guess that's something."

I sighed. "Yes, it's something. She isn't out of danger yet, but the surgeon seemed optimistic. We won't be able to see her until tomorrow, so we came home."

"We're at the beach with all the kids. I can bring them home when we're done here."

"Actually, Zak and I are going over to the sheriff's office to observe an interview with Elvis #7. If you wouldn't mind keeping the kids until after we're finished with that, that would be wonderful."

"I'm happy to help in any way I can," Ellie assured me. "Levi and I will bring the kids to your place and stay there with them if you aren't home yet. They're having fun, so Levi's going to pick up burgers and bring them back for us to have a picnic. We'll probably be here until after sunset."

"Okay, thanks. I appreciate your help. I have our dinner in the oven; I should go check on it. I'll text you if it looks like we won't be home by nine."

By the time I hung up, Zak had come down. We went ahead and ate before I hurried upstairs to take my own shower. I really hoped we were right about what had happened, and that Elvis #7 would be willing to corroborate it. With the conclusion of the competition, we were pretty much out of time. If we didn't get our answers today I wasn't sure we ever would.

Chapter 13

At the sheriff's office we were shown into a small room that was divided from another small room by a mirrored window. The man who was brought in wasn't dressed as Elvis but in regular clothing. I supposed it made sense he would have changed into jeans and a T-shirt now that the competition was over and the competitors were all back to being regular guys rather than the king of rock and roll, even whoever the winner was. I wondered who that was. I didn't really care that much, but I'd met several of the contestants and admitted to being curious.

"Can you tell me why I'm here?" Connor Brown demanded after Deputy Buckner joined him in the small room.

"I have some questions for you regarding the death of Calvin Jobs."

Brown went pale.

"I understand you were staying in the motel room next to Mr. Jobs during the past week," Buckner continued.

"Yeah. So?"

"I also understand your room and his were connected by a door that could provide a suite."

He shrugged. "Maybe. I didn't notice. In case you aren't in the loop, I was part of a competition this weekend. A very demanding and high-profile competition. What that means is that I was busy. Very, very, busy. I didn't have time to notice things like extra doors."

Buckner leaned back in his chair. "I understand you had a busy week. I also have information that suggests you and Mr. Jobs were not only rivals but enemies as well. It appears that of all the contestants, you had the most reason to kill him."

Brown shook his head. "Calvin and I were friends. We were rivals, but certainly not enemies. I didn't have a problem with him and I certainly didn't kill anyone."

Buckner eyed Brown up and down. It seemed to make him squirm, which was probably the point. We'd discussed claiming to have evidence as a means of getting him to confess to helping Calvin fake his own death, so I imagined the long pause was his way of leading up to it. The deputy cleared his throat and narrowed his gaze. "You said you didn't notice the door that connected the two rooms?"

"That's right. I was only in my room to sleep."

"That's interesting, because we found evidence to suggest you used that door to access Mr. Jobs's room."

"What evidence?" Brown demanded.

"Your fingerprints were on both sides of the door as well as on the deadbolt, which can be locked or unlocked from either side."

Brown was beginning to look sick, but he didn't answer.

"We furthermore believe the reason you accessed the room was to put a knife in Mr. Jobs's chest while a witness slept nearby."

Even though I knew Buckner was lying, he was very convincing. If I'd been the one being interrogated I'd have been sweating too.

"I didn't kill Calvin." The guy looked like he was going to burst into tears. "I swear to you."

"So you're saying you didn't access Mr. Jobs's room through the connecting door?" Buckner asked.

"No, I'm not saying that. I did go into Calvin's room through the connecting door. But I didn't kill him."

"If not to kill him, why did you access the room?" Buckner asked. "Keep in mind, one of the prints we found was bloody."

Brown let out a long groan. "It wasn't supposed to go down the way it did. I was just trying to help, but everything went wrong."

"Explain," Buckner demanded.

Connor Brown hung his head. He ran his hands through his hair. I could see he was struggling with a decision. Eventually, he began to speak. "Calvin got himself into trouble with some bad people."

"What kind of trouble?" Buckner asked.

"He worked for this guy who ran a jewel theft ring. I don't know all the details, but basically, he was paid to smuggle gems through customs by replacing the fake ones on his jackets with the real thing. At first it was small jobs, replacing one or two stones at a time that could easily be hidden among all the fake stuff, but then the guy got more demanding, and

Calvin felt the risk to him was increasing out of hand. He wanted out, but the guy wouldn't let him go, so he came up with the idea of faking his own death."

Brown paused.

"Go on," Deputy Buckner encouraged.

"Calvin couldn't pull off the stunt alone, so he paid me twenty grand to help him. We had a good plan, or at least it seemed like we did."

"Describe the plan in detail, starting from the beginning."

"I'll do my best." Brown tapped his chin, as if that would engage his memory. "We knew for it to work we'd need a believable witness. We wouldn't be able to provide a body, but we figured if we had a witness who actually saw Calvin dead, the cops would investigate. It had to be someone who didn't already know Calvin, so we decided to look for a target in town after the fireworks show on the Fourth. We ended up in a bar with a whole lot of other people. Calvin lucked out and found a senior woman he thought would make a convincing witness, then struck up a conversation with her. I invited them both to a party where Calvin could get her liquored up and check her out as a possibility. He asked her back to his room and gave her a little something to make her sleep in her drink. He set the scene with the fake knife and the fake blood. Calvin said the drug he gave the old dame would wear off after four or five hours. The plan was for me to wait until he knocked on the connecting door, letting me know she was coming around, and he'd get into place. When I heard the knock I was supposed to crack the connecting door and wait for her to come to."

"Is that what you did?" Buckner asked.

He nodded. "I responded with my own knock when I heard Calvin's, then waited about five minutes. I cracked the door open to make sure Calvin was in place on the bed next to the old woman. Then I watched some TV while I waited for her to begin to stir. It took longer than I thought it would, but I had nothing else going on, so it was fine."

"So you weren't watching the woman the entire time?" Buckner asked.

"No. Like I said, I was watching the television, but I kept an ear out for the scream I was expecting to come from the next room."

Buckner made a few notes. "Okay, then what?"

"My job was to go into the room just after the dame woke up and found Calvin dead so I could take control of the situation. I would be the one to call 911. I was supposed to be the hero and cover for her. I'd convince her the police would suspect her of killing Calvin, but I'd send her on her way, tell her I'd take the fall."

"What if she didn't leave?" Buckner asked.

"If I couldn't get her to go, I had photos of her with Calvin from the night before. If she hung around the police would definitely think she killed him. I guess there still wasn't a guarantee she'd leave, but if she didn't, I'd have figured something out. As it turned out, the old dame bolted before I could make my move, so I didn't need to do any of that."

"Okay, so the witness leaves the room and then what?"

"The plan was for Calvin to disappear."

"So where did Mr. Jobs go after he left Ashton Falls and how can we reach him now?" Deputy Buckner asked.

"He didn't leave and you can't reach him."

"What do you mean, he didn't leave? He wasn't in the room when Ms. Zimmerman returned with her grandmother and he hasn't been seen all week."

"What I meant was that he didn't leave Ashton Falls as planned. He did leave the room, but only because I moved him on account of him being dead."

I gasped. Dead?

Buckner frowned. "Perhaps you should give me a few more details."

Brown crossed his arms on the table in front of him. "As I said, the plan was for Calvin to disappear once the old woman saw him dead on the bed. When she took off on that pink Harley of hers, I made a comment about things going as planned, but Calvin didn't say anything. When he didn't move after a few more minutes I tried to rouse him, but he was deader than a doornail."

"How did he die?" Buckner asked.

Brown shrugged. "Beats me. He looked fine. Physically, I mean. He didn't have any gunshot wounds or anything. He looked real peaceful. Like he was sleeping."

"And where's the body now?"

Connor Brown hesitated. "Is it against the law to bury a body even if you absolutely aren't responsible for it being dead?"

"Yes, it is."

"Dang. Guess I should have done things a little different. I wasn't trying to hurt anyone or break any laws. I was just trying to help a friend. I think maybe I might have made a mess of things."

I looked at Zak with what I was sure was an expression of shock on my face. Talk about a twist. A man cooked up an elaborate scheme to fake his own death only to end up dead? I wondered why. And I wondered whether someone had killed him or if he'd had a heart attack and faded away. I tapped on the glass. I knew I wasn't supposed to do that, but I had a question I wanted to be sure was answered.

Buckner excused himself and came into the room where Zak and I were waiting. "I told you not to do that."

"I know. But I wanted to be sure you asked about Calvin's possessions. His luggage, and especially his costumes."

"You think someone killed him to get the costumes?"

"It makes sense," I pointed out.

"Maybe, but the timing is off. Jobs knocked on the door to let Brown know Nona was waking up. He got into place. If he died at that point, there was no way a third party could have come into the room."

"Maybe, but just ask. The costumes feel like the key to figuring everything out."

"Okay, I'll ask. But from now on, remember that waiting quietly means waiting quietly."

Buckner returned to the interrogation room. He asked my question as promised, along with a bunch of others relating to Calvin Jobs's death.

"So after you tried to wake Jobs and found out he was actually dead, what did you do?" Buckner asked Brown.

"First, I freaked out. I mean, like big-time meltdown. Here I was, wanting to help the guy have a second start in life and he was dead? How could that have happened? It made no sense. I didn't see or hear a struggle of any kind. How can a man just lay down and die?"

"An autopsy should tell us that. What I'd like to know is what you did after you found him dead?"

"After I finished freaking out I knew I had to move and move quickly, so I wrapped Calvin in the plastic he'd put down under the sheet to protect the mattress from the fake blood, then moved him into my room. I traded out the bloody sheets on his bed with my own clean ones."

"So you must have done all this before Ms. Zimmerman arrived with her grandmother."

Brown nodded. "Once I made the decision to move Calvin I was real quick. By the time the old dame showed up with her granddaughter, the room was as spotless as it would have been if no one had ever been there."

Buckner steepled his fingers. "Okay, so you moved the body through the connecting door into your own room after wrapping it in plastic. Then what?"

"Then I waited for nightfall. When it was dark I transferred the body to my car, then took it into the woods and buried it."

"Do you remember where you buried it?" Deputy Buckner asked.

He nodded. "I can find the spot."

"Okay. So after you buried the body, then what?"

"Then nothing. I went to the competition and tried to act normal. I figured by the time anyone found Calvin's body, if they ever did, I'd be long gone."

"What about the sheets?"

"I dumped them along with Calvin's blue jacket earlier that morning. Both had the fake blood on them, so I drove across town and tossed them in a dumpster."

Buckner leaned in just a bit. I hoped he was getting to my question. "What about Calvin's personal possessions? What did you do with those?"

"Nothing. Calvin's costumes and other personal things were in the room before the rehearsal that evening. I saw them there while we finalized the plan. But by the time I came into the room the next morning to fulfill my part, all of his possessions, including his costumes, were gone."

"So who took them and why?"

Brown shrugged. "I have no idea."

I glanced at Zak. "I have a feeling this mystery isn't quite as over as we'd like it to be."

"I was thinking the same thing."

I continued. "Either Calvin moved his things before putting the plan into action or someone stole them while he was out partying. If his possessions were stolen, it seems that should have given him enough pause to abandon the plan. The only other time the costumes could have been stolen was after Nona and Calvin got to the room but before Brown was brought into play. But if Calvin was in the room when his belongings were removed, wouldn't he have made a fuss about it? If he had, someone would have heard something."

"Which means Calvin must have moved his belongings himself as part of the plan to disappear quickly."

I frowned. "Yeah, I guess."

After the interview Buckner followed Brown's directions and found Calvin's body right where he said he'd buried it. It was dug up and transferred to the ME's office so he could determine the cause of death. Connor Brown was arrested for crimes related to concealing a body and burying it on land that belonged to the National Forest Service. I wasn't sure what would happen with him, but I was more interested in what had happened to Calvin and where his possessions were. At least we had corroboration of what had happened to Nona, which should help her deal with it.

It was late by the time we got home and we were exhausted. We fell into bed and a dreamless sleep, at least for a few hours. When I woke in a cold sweat at four a.m. I knew I was going to need to find out the rest of the story, even if I could already deliver the answers to Nona we'd set out to find.

Chapter 14

Monday, July 9

"If Nona remembered seeing Calvin's possessions when she arrived in his room, and they were gone by the time she and I returned to find the body gone, they had to have been removed either by Calvin while Nona slept or by someone else after he was dead," I said to Zak as we drove to Bryton Lake that morning. "Connor Brown indicated the possessions were gone when he went into the room to find Calvin dead, so unless he's lying and he really took them, it only makes sense that Calvin himself removed them, or perhaps he had another accomplice who came by and picked everything up after Nona passed out."

"Okay, say that's true," Zak responded as he turned the wheel of his truck into a tight S curve. "If Calvin cleared his room of his possessions in preparation for a quick exit, which really does make sense, where did he stash them? Did he have a car? I don't remember a vehicle being mentioned at any point."

I tilted my head. Zak had asked a good question. "We know he went to the bar, but he showed up with a group, so he might have gotten a ride. We also know he and Nona went to a party at the beach, but I seem to remember Nona saying they'd taken her bike back to the motel. We should ask her, if she's in any shape to answer questions, that is." I frowned. "I wonder if she'll be able to speak. I wonder if she'll even know who we are. I imagine we should anticipate some pretty significant side effects after brain surgery."

Zak's lips tightened. I could see he was as worried as I was about what those side effects might turn out to be.

I decided to change the subject back to the Elvis mystery. Worrying about what we might find once we reached the hospital wasn't going to help anyone. "I thought I'd call Deputy Buckner later. I'm hoping he'll have at least a preliminary autopsy report. I'm very interested to find out if Calvin died of natural causes while he was lying there on the bed pretending to be dead, which would be beyond crazy, of if someone slipped in and killed him during the five minutes between when Calvin knocked on the door to alert Brown that he was ready to put the fake death scene into play and cracked open the door."

"The odds of either happening is pretty small," Zak said as he came to a stop at the light at the bottom of the mountain. "The only thing that makes any sense is that Brown killed him."

"I agree, but if he did, why would he even mention the fact that he was dead to Buckner? Everyone assumed Calvin just took off."

Zak made a left turn onto the highway leading to Bryton Lake. "It doesn't make sense he would have. Maybe there was a third person involved. I can't remember if Buckner asked Brown about anyone else who might have been in on the plan."

"I'll ask him when I call him. Do you think we should stop to get flowers for Nona?"

"She's in Intensive Care, so she can't have flowers. Once they move her to a room we'll get her the biggest bouquet we can find."

My heart was pounding a million miles an hour while Zak and I waited to speak to a doctor before being allowed to visit Nona. I figured the news must be of the bad variety; otherwise why not send a nurse to fill us in? I thought I was prepared for anything, but the longer we waited, the more certain I became that the short- or long-term side effects we could expect would be terrifying.

"Mr. and Mrs. Zimmerman," the doctor greeted us. "Your grandmother is awake and stable. We're going to keep her in ICU for a couple of days to make sure there are no complications, but we don't anticipate any problems."

I let out a breath of relief.

"Your grandmother will need full-time care when she leaves here. If you or another friend or relative aren't able to provide it, I can recommend a long-term care facility."

"She'll come home with us," I said immediately. "I'll take care of her." I glanced at Zak. "We both will."

The doctor smiled. "I'm happy to hear that. We find our patients do much better at home."

"Are there any significant side effects we need to be aware of?" Zak asked.

I put my hand on his leg and he wrapped my hand in his while we waited for the doctor's reply.

"Your grandmother is a strong woman who did very well considering the invasive nature of both the tumor and the surgery to remove it. There may be some memory loss, especially short-term memory. It's hard to know at this point because she's still pretty groggy. Additionally, her balance might be affected, at least in the short term. I recommend that you rent a wheelchair for her to get around until she's steady on her feet. We spoke briefly, and her speech seems fine, although, again, she's a bit groggy. What she says might not make a whole lot of sense."

"Anything else we should know?" I asked.

"A nurse will go over everything with you prior to release. If you plan to care for her yourself, we'll be certain you know exactly what to do and what to look for. The nurse out front will show you to her bed, but we're going to limit the visit to just five minutes today. You can come back tomorrow and every day after that, if you'd like, but I don't want her to overdo."

Zak and I held hands as we followed the nurse down the hall. I wanted to cry when I saw all the machines Nona was hooked up to and the turban wrapped around her head. She looked small and weak, but at least she was alive. I had exactly zero experience being a nurse, but I figured I could learn what I didn't know so Nona would receive the best care and get back to her old self as soon as possible.

"How are you feeling?" I asked as I sat down next to Nona's bed. Zak stood next to me. We'd been told to be careful of all the tubes and wires, so I sat with my hands in my lap, even though I wanted to hug the poor, frail woman.

"Been better," Nona croaked out. "You here to take me home?"

I glanced at Zak.

"Not today, Nona. The doctor wants to make sure all your vitals are stable before he'll release you. But Zoe and I will come back every day, and as soon as we get the all clear, we'll take you home and get you settled into your suite."

"I don't want to be a bother."

Zak touched her hand with one of his fingers. "You could never be a bother. We love you and are happy to have you stay with us for as long as necessary."

Nona closed her eyes. It looked like she might have dozed off. Zak motioned to me that we should probably leave. We were only supposed to stay a few minutes anyway.

"You catch Elvis's killer?" Nona asked as I stood.

I decided to keep it simple. "Not yet. But we're close. Really close. I should have news by tomorrow."

"I heard something," Nona said. "As I was coming to. I'd forgotten about it, but it came to me all of a sudden as I was coming out of the anesthesia, which was an eerily similar feeling."

"What did you hear?"

"I think there was someone else in the room. I wasn't all the way awake yet and everything felt blurred and fragmented, but I remember hearing the

147

door close. I think I fell back asleep for a few minutes at least before I came to all the way, but I remember the scent of strawberries. Of course, smelling things that aren't there could be a symptom of the brain tumor they just removed."

"Maybe. But it might be an important clue as well," I answered, just as the nurse came in and indicated we needed to leave. "We'll be back tomorrow, hopefully with the answers you're looking for."

Zak kissed Nona on the forehead and we followed the nurse out of the cubicle, down the hallway, and out of the ICU.

"I know who killed Calvin," I said as we walked through the hospital to the parking area.

"Who?"

"A woman I met at the competition. I don't know her name, but I sure as heck intend to find out."

******

The woman I'd spoken to on the beach last Friday had sported red hair and smelled like strawberries. She'd told me that she'd been following the Elvises for a long time and had taken the time to speak to and get to know them all. She also was the one who'd first mentioned to me that Calvin had all his costumes custom made. I had no idea why she'd kill Elvis #3, but if Nona smelled strawberries in his motel room, I was pretty sure that woman had been there. I wondered how she'd pulled it off. Maybe she'd been there all along. Maybe Calvin had taken Nona back to the room and drugged her, then found himself in want of some female companionship. Maybe she'd been hanging around and he'd invited her in, or perhaps her being in the room was her idea and she'd knocked on his door. Maybe she'd slipped Calvin some of the drug he'd given Nona, or maybe she'd had a drug of her own. Maybe she waited until he fell asleep and then killed him. Or maybe she knew about the plan from the beginning. Maybe she'd been the one to knock on the door to alert Connor Brown that Nona was waking before she left. There were certainly a lot of maybes, but I was determined to turn all of them into answers by the end of the day.

I called Buckner while Zak drove back up the mountain. He was willing to talk with us, so we arranged to meet him at his office when we arrived back in town. I hoped that between my hunch about the strawberry redhead and the results of the autopsy, we'd finally be able to put this mystery to bed.

Chapter 15

Buckner was waiting for us when we arrived at the sheriff's office. I jumped right in with what Nona had remembered when she was in and out of consciousness in the motel room. I also shared that I'd met a woman on the beach with red hair who smelled like strawberries.

"Is this the woman you saw?" Buckner slid a photo across the desk.

I nodded. "Yes, that's her. Who is she?"

"Her name is Bonnie Needlemeyer. A couple of witnesses remembered seeing her hanging around the motel the night Calvin Jobs died. No one thought anything about it until I started asking questions. It seems she was a regular with the Elvis crowd. She even followed them from state to state."

"Do you know where she is now?"

"Seattle."

I frowned. "I guess it makes sense she wouldn't still be here now that the contest is over. In fact, I never saw her again after that one time, so she may have left early. Are you going to have Seattle PD arrest her?"

"I've already had them bring her in for questioning. She claims to have been a part of Calvin's plan, that after Nona passed out, Calvin texted her and she came over. He put his belongings in the car she'd rented because he'd gotten a ride to Ashton Falls with another Elvis. She'd agreed to drive both him and his belongings out of town after his fake-death drama had played out. She helped him with the fake blood and knife as Nona was beginning to come to, then left. He'd told her he'd meet her in a parking lot a few blocks away once he was done. He never showed. She heard he'd taken off and didn't know he was dead, so she figured he'd reneged on the money he'd promised her and cut her out of the deal. She wasn't too upset because she had the costumes, which she figured he no longer needed and she could sell for a pretty penny."

"So he never showed and she just went on about her business?" I asked.

"She said she went to visit her sister, who lives in Bryton Lake, for a few days before flying home."

I took a deep breath and tried to make sense of that. "So who killed Calvin?"

"Actually, I believe Ms. Needlemeyer did. The autopsy report shows he died from heart failure brought on by a drug cocktail injected directly into his heart. There was a small puncture wound in his chest. The logical assumption is that Ms. Needlemeyer helped set up the scene for the fake death as planned, then administered the drugs. He would have died almost immediately."

"So is she going to be charged with Calvin's death?"

Buckner shook his head. "At this point all we have is a theory, and Ms. Needlemeyer isn't 'fessing up. The Seattle PD are working on her. There is one other possibility, though. Two, in fact. One is that Conner Brown killed Jobs, which in my opinion seems unlikely. The other is that the man you captured in your photo killed Jobs and was in the room the whole time."

"Did you ever find out who that was?"

"No, but we have witnesses who saw a tall man with dark hair and a long, pointy nose hanging around earlier in the day."

"A tall man with a pointy nose?" I said. "The man who approached me that day was tall and had a pointy nose. He said he was from the costume company and was there to collect Calvin's costumes. He thought someone from the contest had them because he'd left. He must have killed Calvin so he could steal the costumes, which I'm betting he knew had real gems sewn onto them."

Buckner frowned. "You think the real stones were still sewn onto the costumes? It seems an unnecessary risk to bring them to the competition."

"Maybe, but what if Calvin knew he was going to disappear and wanted them to help him make a new start? He wouldn't want to carry around a bag of gems that would most likely have been flagged at the airport, so he left his last shipment on the costumes rather than turning them over to whoever he'd stolen them for. He planned to fake his death and take off with them, but somehow his boss found out what he planned and sent the tall man with the pointy nose to deal with Calvin and collect the gems. Do you know if Ms. Needlemeyer still had Calvin's stuff?"

"She did. The Seattle PD are collecting it. If she killed him, we'll figure out a way to prove it."

******

I provided the sketch artist with an image of the tall man with the pointy nose, then Zak and I left the sheriff's office. We still didn't know for certain who had killed Calvin, but Buckner said he'd call me when he had news and there wasn't a lot we could do to help. We'd let the police do their jobs while we spent time with our family. We felt bad that we'd had to postpone sailing yet again, so we invited everyone over for a BBQ and swim party. In addition to the Dentons, we asked my parents and Harper and my grandfather and his girlfriend, Hazel, to join us.

"I'd like to make an announcement," my grandfather, Luke Donovan, said after we'd finished eating. He glanced at Hazel, who sat beside him. She smiled and nodded. "Hazel and I are getting hitched."

"You're getting married?" I chirped with happiness. "Congratulations." I got up and hugged both Grandpa and Hazel, and pretty much everyone else did likewise. "When?" I asked after the commotion calmed down a bit.

"In a couple of weeks," Grandpa answered.

"Couple of weeks?" My mom was the one chirping this time. "You can't plan a wedding in a couple of weeks."

"Sure you can, if you keep it small," Grandpa countered. "We already spoke to the reverend and we plan to invite only family and a few close friends."

I wanted to argue, but Zak squeezed my hand in a gesture I was sure was to remind me that this was, after all, their wedding. "I think that sounds perfect. You can have it here." I glanced at my mother. "Mom and I will help with whatever you need."

"I'll help too," Alex, who was standing next to Hazel, added.

"We're keeping it casual," Hazel said. "Very casual. But a few friends to witness the ceremony and then a simple meal on the deck would be nice."

Mom and Ellie started batting around ideas while Hazel, probably against her better judgment, became swept up in things.

"Do you think they'll end up with the simple ceremony they want?" Levi whispered in my ear after he slid over next to me.

"Probably not. But I'm staying out of it. I'll happily do whatever I'm asked, but this is their day and I'm going to respect whatever they decide."

"You're going to have a lot on your plate, taking care of Nona and helping to plan the wedding," Levi said.

"Yeah. I may have to ask Jeremy if he's willing to come back to the Zoo a week early. I can't leave Aspen there all alone. She knows what to do, but it's a lot for one person to handle day after day."

"Seems like that's what she's been doing this past week," Levi pointed out.

"True. But I hate to ask her to do the work of three people for any longer than she already has."

"I'll go in and help her," Levi offered.

I turned with a look of surprise. "Really? You would do that?"

Levi shrugged. "Sure. I'm off until football practice starts in August and I'm getting antsy with so much time on my hands. I've helped you out before, so I have a general understanding of what needs to be done. Plus Aspen will be there if I have questions and I can always call you."

I hugged Levi. "Thank you so much. You really are the best friend."

Levi grinned. "Something to keep in mind when my birthday rolls around."

I punched him playfully in the arm. "I already know what I'm getting you for your birthday and it's going to be great."

"I'm sure it will be." Levi hugged me back. "Your pocket is ringing."

I pulled out my phone. "It's Buckner. I'm going to take this inside."

Once I got away from the crowd I answered. "Do you have news?"

"We identified the tall man with the pointy nose from the sketch. His name is Warren Greenway and he has a record. A thick one. The feds are taking over the case, at least temporarily. I have a feeling Interpol may get involved, given the international flavor of things."

"Did he kill Calvin?"

"I'm giving the feds all the information I have to do with as they see fit, but my money is still on Bonnie Needlemeyer as the killer, though we found the gems in her apartment, but she's still holding to her story that she was transporting Calvin's possessions with his permission and she didn't kill him."

"Yet she conveniently kept the gems he had in his possession."

"Like I said, my money is on her."

Chapter 16

Saturday, July 28

I felt a tear slide down my cheek as Grandpa and Hazel exchanged vows they'd written themselves for the small ceremony witnessed by family and friends. I was somewhat surprised we'd managed to keep it small, but Hazel had insisted on handling the guest list and Mom and I had agreed she should have everyone she wanted and no one she didn't. Having lived in Ashton Falls as long as she had, keeping the guest list to less than fifty must have been difficult. She'd asked her good friend Phyllis King to stand up with her, and Grandpa had chosen Ethan Carlton to be his best man. It seemed Grandpa and Hazel and Ethan and Phyllis, had been hanging out as a foursome quite a bit lately. Ethan and Phyllis weren't officially dating, but it didn't take a genius to notice the shy glances and gentle touches the two exchanged throughout the afternoon.

Alex and Ellie had taken on the task of providing the meal, which was enjoyed by all. Mom and Phyllis had helped Hazel with her dress and hair, and Levi and Scooter had taken over baby and Nona duty, while Zak helped my dad and Ethan get Grandpa ready. I was in charge of getting Harper ready for flower girl duty, as well as making sure the flower arrangements had been set out just as Hazel had instructed. Eli wasn't quite old enough to fulfill the role of ring bearer, so Charlie was awarded the job, and I have to say he fulfilled his role like a pro.

The day was bright and sunny, a mild sixty-eight, so not too hot. The air was still and the lake glassy as everyone gathered around to support the couple as they took their first steps toward beginning a new and hopefully long life together. After the ceremony, Jeremy and his band played show tunes as requested, while Jeremy's wife, Jessica, kept an eye on her daughter Rosalie, his daughter Morgan, and their daughter Emma, a name that, they told us, meant whole or complete, which was exactly what their family now was.

"If I knew you were having a party I would have worn my dress uniform."

"Salinger," I screeched as I hugged the man who'd come into the kitchen while I was helping to serve the food. "I'm so glad you're back. Did you find yourself?"

Sheriff Salinger laughed. "I think I did."

"I can't believe you left without telling me. You know how I depend on you."

Salinger shrugged. "I figured now you were retired from the sleuthing business, we wouldn't be working together anymore."

I handed the sheriff a large bowl of macaroni salad to carry out to the buffet table. "Well, apparently this retirement thing isn't working out as expected. Deputy Buckner was great, he really was, but I missed you." I set my bowl on the table and motioned for Salinger to set the one he was carrying beside it. "Did you hear about the wedding or just stop by to let me know you were back?"

"Neither. Who got married?"

"My grandpa and Hazel. It was very sudden, but I couldn't be happier for them."

Salinger smiled. "Good for them. There are those who would say they're too old to start over again."

"And they'd be wrong."

"Can we talk in private for a minute?" Salinger asked, a slightly more serious expression on his face.

"Sure. Let's go into Zak's office. No one will bother us there."

As soon as we were settled, Salinger said, "I have good news and bad news. Which do you want first?"

I grimaced. "I guess the bad."

"I heard from your friend Shredder. He wanted to let me know that Claudia is still in the wind." Claudia Lotherman was a criminal master of disguise who had become my archnemesis. Not only had she tried to kill me when Zak and I were in Alaska and again before my wedding, but just a few months ago she'd kidnapped Zak and made me jump through hoops to get him back. Shredder, a mysterious man Zak and I had met while in Hawaii, who was some sort of a spy, or special ops guy, or possibly with some other supersecret group or organization, was almost as smart as Zak and had connections that seemed to know no limits. He'd helped me with the recent Claudia situation and had been on her tail ever since.

"That's unfortunate, but I wouldn't necessarily say it's bad news."

"Maybe and maybe not. The reason he called was to give me a heads-up that Claudia could be heading back in our direction."

I narrowed my gaze. "Why would she risk that when she knows everyone is looking for her?"

Salinger shrugged. "The woman's crazy. And fearless. Not a good combination."

"No," I agreed. "I guess not."

"Shredder doesn't have any concrete evidence that she's coming this way, he just wanted me to keep an eye on things. She'll be less likely to pull one over on us again if we know she might be around sometime soon."

"True. Am I ever thankful he's monitoring the situation." The very idea that Claudia might be heading in this direction filled me with terror, but I couldn't do a thing about it and didn't want to dwell on it. "You said you had good news too?"

"They arrested Bonnie Needlemeyer in the Calvin Jobs murder. As it turned out, Warren Greenway, the man your photo happened to capture, was watching the motel room all night, looking for an opportunity to break in and steal the gems. He saw Ms. Needlemeyer toss something into a dumpster after she left Jobs's room. He checked it out and found the syringe she used to kill him. He held on to it just in case he had a reason to use it for his own purposes."

"So she absolutely did it?"

"She still hasn't confessed, but it looks like she's the killer you've been after. And Greenway confessed, as part of a larger plea deal, to being part of the jewel theft ring Calvin was involved with. From what I understand, Interpol is closing in on the entire operation."

I grinned. "That *is* good news. I'm sure Nona will rest easier knowing this whole thing is wrapped up."

"How is she? I heard what happened."

"Remarkably well, considering. She's out on the deck if you want to go by to say hi."

"I don't want to keep you from your party. We can catch up later."

I put my arm through Salinger's. "Come and have some food. Ellie's been cooking all week. I can guarantee we'll need help eating it."

******

Later that evening, Zak and I snuggled with Catherine and Charlie in our suite. It had been a fantastic day and everyone, including Nona, had had a wonderful time. We still hadn't broached the subject of her moving in with us on a permanent basis, but she was comfortable in her suite and seemed happy. There was time to talk about it when she brought up the subject.

I hadn't told Zak about Claudia, mostly because I didn't want to worry him. I'd tell him, just not today.

"Did you notice Alex and Diego holding hands during the ceremony?" Zak asked, as he got up from the sofa where we'd been sitting and moved to the rocking chair with Catherine.

"I did. It was sweet. I know they're young, but I really like Diego. He helped me save you. He's a good kid."

Zak scowled. "She's only thirteen."

"She's almost fourteen and old enough to want to have a boy in her life. Would you rather have her crushing on someone else?"

"I'd rather have her not crushing on anyone. Scooter is thirteen too, and he isn't the least bit interested in girls."

"Alex is a lot more mature than Scooter. It's only natural that her intellect and emotional maturity would put her ahead of the curve in other areas as well."

Zak continued to frown.

"You don't need to worry about Alex," I continued. "She isn't a pushover and she has a good head on her shoulders. Besides, Diego seems to be a perfect gentleman."

"Perfect gentlemen are the ones you have to watch out for the most," Zak countered.

I glanced at the look of adoration Zak had on his face as he rocked Catherine. The poor thing. If Zak was this protective with Alex, I couldn't imagine how overprotective he was going to be with her. She probably wouldn't be allowed to date until she was thirty. If ever.

"Looks like she's asleep," Zak said as he stroked her cheek. "I'll put her down, then wash up for bed."

"I'm going to check on the other kids, then be back. Don't forget to plug the baby monitor back in. I had it downstairs earlier."

Zak stood up slowly so he wouldn't disturb Catherine. "Will do."

I found Alex in her room, playing with the four kittens I'd rescued. They'd grown a lot and all seemed healthy. Unfortunately, we'd never found the mom. I'd begin looking for forever homes for them when they were around eight weeks old. Scooter was in his room with Digger and the dog he was fostering, Gus. I'd seen Barney, who was doing a lot better. The doctor thought he could go back home in another week or so. Scooter had been doing a good job with Gus, and I knew he'd been having a nice stay with us, but I was sure he'd be as happy to get home as Barney.

I saw Nona's door was open as I passed. She was sitting in the dark, looking out the window. "Nona." I knocked once.

"Come in, dear," Nona said without turning around.

"Are you okay? Do you need anything?"

"I'm fine," she assured me. "Just mulling over a few things. I think better in the dark."

I sat down on a chair near her. "I get that. Fewer distractions. Are you sure there isn't something I can help you with?"

Nona let out a sigh. "Not really. I was just thinking about the ceremony today. It was lovely."

"It was."

"Did it feel at all odd to you, watching your grandfather marry someone who wasn't your grandmother?"

"Not at all. I loved my grandmother very much, but she's been gone a long time. I'm very happy my grandfather found someone to live out his life with. And I love Hazel. I adored her even before Grandpa did. I think they're going to be very happy together."

"I'm sure they will," Nona said in a soft voice. "It's hard being alone when the spouse you chose to spend your life with dies long before you."

I moved closer to Nona and took her hand in mine. "I've heard Zak talk about your husband, but I'm not sure I've ever heard him say how long ago he passed."

"A long time ago. I loved him, although we didn't get along all that well. I guess what I miss most is having someone to talk to and share a meal with at the end of the day."

"You have us," I answered. "It might not be the same thing, but Zak and I and Alex and Scooter and even Catherine absolutely adore you. We want you to stay here with us. Permanently."

Nona turned and looked at me. "That's very kind, dear, but you have three kids and half a dozen animals here. The last thing you need is a crazy old woman underfoot."

I smiled. "I like crazy. In fact, I think having a little crazy in your life is an absolute necessity. Zak and I love you. You're family. We really want you to stay."

Nona didn't answer, but I could see her eyes had grown heavy with unshed tears.

"At least think about it," I added. "I know you value your freedom, but Zak and I plan to have a whole litter of babies before we're done. We're going to need help with all those babies. If you aren't interested in staying, we'll need to hire someone to do it."

Nona wiped away one of the tears that had managed to escape. "You really need my help?"

I stood up and hugged the frail-feeling woman. "We absolutely need your help. Will you do it? Will you stay and help Zak and me raise our family?"

Tears streamed down Nona's face. "I'd love that."

Coming next from Kathi Daley Books

Preview Chapter 1

Monday, June 11

Some secrets are meant to be shared, others are better off forgotten.

Sixteen-year-old Naomi Collins disappeared on April 12, 2002. She'd been a troubled teen living in a dysfunctional home, and most people assumed she'd simply run away to start a new life in a new town under an assumed name. In theory, I suppose that made sense. Based on the information I'd been able to dig up, Naomi had been brought up in a home fraught with alcoholism, abuse, and long periods of abandonment. She was the only child of a hard, sadistic man, a fisherman by trade, who, according to witnesses, beat and berated his weak and timid wife whenever the mood struck.

Shortly before Naomi disappeared, her mother suffered a nervous breakdown and was voluntarily admitted to a psychiatric facility. Naomi was left alone with her father, who, it was said, spent more time in the local pub than at home. Naomi was an average student who seemed to enjoy school, although she had few friends. I assumed that was a byproduct of her father's refusal to allow her to engage in social activities other than an occasional event sponsored by the high school.

So, why, you might ask, if this missing persons case seemed to be cut and dried, would I spend an entire week of my six-week vacation in the seaside town of Cutter's Cove, investigating some random girl who'd lived in town before I'd ever set foot on the sandy shore of the majestic Oregon coast? The answer to this understandable question began, as so many events in my life have, with a dream.

"You're up early," Mom said when she joined me on the deck of the mansion she and I had renovated when we first lived in Cutter's Cove. The historic home was not only magnificent structurally but perched on a bluff overlooking the Pacific Ocean. It was the perfect place to while away a lazy day.

"Couldn't sleep," I answered with a yawn as I watched seagulls glide over the aqua ocean, searching for their morning meal.

"I'm sorry to hear that," Mom sympathized as she sat down on a lounge chair next to me. We both sipped our coffee from sturdy ceramic mugs as we waited, along with my dogs Tucker and Sunny, for the sun to peek its brilliant head over the horizon. It was nice to be here in this place together again after so many years. Mom had I had first moved to Cutter's Cove Twelve years ago after I witnessed a gangland shooting that landed my mother and me in the witness protection program. I thought the transition would be difficult, and it was, at first. But then I met my new best friends, Trevor Johnson and Mackenzie Reynolds, and suddenly, a middle-class life didn't seem so bad. For two years, I lived in Cutter's Cove,

Oregon, as Alyson, the seemingly out of the blue, the murderers I had run from were eliminated by their own family, and my new life in Cutter's Cove was no longer a necessity. After a long discussion, Mom and I decided to go back to New York, where I went to college and, after graduation, went on to work for a top advertising firm as a graphic artist. Mom bought an estate in the country and, for the most part, we were happy. Still, there was a part of me that would always belong to Cutter's Cove. I just didn't know how literal that actually was.

"Are you feeling all right?" Mom asked.

I reached my arms over my head, yawned again, and let out a long sigh. "I'm fine. It's just the dream I've been having for the past few days that's been keeping me awake."

"Dream?" Mom asked as she turned toward me and angled her head slightly to the side.

"It's a long story," I said, and I realized my fatigue was evident in my voice. I leaned back, closed my eyes, and ran my fingers through Sunny's long black fur as the waves crashing in the distance soothed me.

"I'd like to help. Especially if you feel this is more than a simple dream. Do you think it's a portent?"

I opened my eyes and momentarily considered my mother. She was one of the few people who knew about my power to both see ghosts and occasionally see glimpses of the future in dream form. She was one of the few people in my life who knew everything about me, the normal and the strange, and never judges. If there was anyone I could always talk to, it was her. "No," I answered, "not a portent exactly. I think I'm being drawn into something that took place in the past." I adjusted my position on the chase so I was sitting up straight rather than leaning back, as I had been. "The dream always starts off with me walking up a long, narrow trail that leads from a parking field of some sort, then climbs up to a bluff overlooking the sea. It's foggy and visibility is limited. Basically, during the walk all I can see is what's directly in front of my feet as I travel. It occurs to me as I make the journey that something's very wrong, and that I should turn back. Yet, despite my own thoughts about doing just that, I continue to walk. It's almost as if I'm being pulled along against my will."

"It sounds frightening."

"Not so much frightening as heavy. I feel as if I'm carrying a great weight, and the farther down the path I go, the more burdened I become. As I continue, I'm aware of a tightness in my chest. My breath comes in gasps and there's a feeling of fear blanketed by a sort of acceptance. When I get to the top of the bluff, the fog clears. I pause to look around. I find not only a gorgeous view but an abandoned gravesite marked only by a handmade wooden cross. The fear I've been experiencing on the hike up is replaced with a deep sorrow that cuts my soul."

"And the gravesite? Do you have a sense of who's buried there?"

I shook my head. "I don't know for certain, but recently, I've been picking up the name Naomi. I did some research and discovered a Naomi Collins disappeared Cutter's Cove sixteen years ago."

"You think the gravesite in your dreams belongs to Naomi Collins?" Mom asked.

I lifted one shoulder. "Maybe. I don't have a sense yet that Naomi is dead necessarily, but I do know she grew up in a very unhappy home. I spoke to Woody," I said, referring to my friend, Officer Woody Baker. "Officially, it's assumed Naomi ran away. And maybe she did. Based on what I've been able to find out, she certainly had reason to. But the more I look into things, the stronger my intuition is that it's Naomi's grave I'm dreaming about."

"Talk to Woody again," Mom suggested. "He can look in the area you sense and find out who, if anyone, is buried there."

"I'd do that, but I don't know where the grave is. I see it in my dream, but though I've tried, I can't figure out the exact location of the bluff in my dream. Woody's already shared with me everything he knows about Naomi, which isn't much."

"Maybe if you have the dream often enough, eventually you'll develop a sense of where the bluff is," Mom offered.

I stretched my long legs out in front of me. "That's what I'm hoping, although I hope it's soon. I'm exhausted. I'm ready for the dreams to stop messing with my sleep." If I was honest, I'd gotten very little sleep since I came back to Cutter's Cove three weeks ago to track down the killer of an old friend.

Mom stood up. "I'll make us some breakfast and you can fill me in on what you know to this point. It's Monday. Do you think Trevor will be by?" Mom was particularly fond of one of my two best friends, Trevor Johnson. "He mentioned coming for breakfast on his day off."

"I'll text him to confirm, but if I know Trev—and I do!—he won't pass up the opportunity for some of your cooking."

Mom smiled. "I enjoy cooking for that boy. He's always so appreciative."

Not really a boy anymore, I thought to myself, but didn't say as much. "We all enjoy your cooking. In fact, I think it's one of the reasons Mac's arranging to come back to town so quickly. She doesn't want to miss out on any of the delicious meals she knows you'll be cooking while we're here."

"Do you know when she plans to arrive?" Mom asked about my other best friend, Mackenzie Reynolds, who currently lived in California.

"Last I heard, she's flying in on Wednesday, but I'll check to make sure her plans haven't changed."

After Mom went inside, I returned my attention to the sea. The sky grew bright as the sun began to poke its head over the horizon. We'd had rain overnight, and the lingering clouds were brilliant with shades of red, orange, pink, and purple. God, how I'd missed this place. Yes, I'd been busy with my life in New York and hadn't dwelled on what I'd left behind, but the longer I was here, where I'd been the happiest, I wondered if I could bear to leave. Mom owned the house, and I more than enough money that I didn't need to work. From that standpoint, staying in Cutter's Cove wouldn't be a problem. But if I decided to stay there were other things to consider. I had a job I enjoyed and a boyfriend I was fond of but probably wouldn't miss. Mom had her own life in New York, and I doubted she'd want to stay here full time, but she'd be welcome to visit as often as she liked.

As each day passed, I wondered more and more whether my life was here in Cutter's Cove with my dogs and my cat, Shadow, and Trevor. California was a short flight away, so Mac would be able to visit often. I didn't know whether Alyson Prescott, the part of me who'd stayed behind in this house when I left Cutter's Cove and was on the outside now that I'd returned for a short visit would somehow magically make her way back inside if I recommitted my life here. When I'd first arrived and found my teenage self running around the house, as if she were a real person, I was less than thrilled, but now that I'd gotten used to her, I think if we eventually reconnected, I'd miss her. I hadn't mentioned the idea of staying to anyone yet. I wanted to come to a firm decision before I did.

"We should take a photo of the sky and the sea," Alyson said, and there she was, as if thinking about her had made her appear, and hopped up on the railing that separated the deck from the sharp drop to the sea below. "It's exceptional this morning. I bet Mom will want to paint it."

"It is an exceptional sunrise." I smiled at the apparition who was in a lot of ways like me yet in many others very different. "Where did you come from? I haven't seen you in days."

Alyson frowned. "Really? It doesn't feel as if I've been away. I think maybe we're beginning to merge for short periods of time."

"Merge?"

"You said you hadn't seen me, but I've known what you saw, felt, even thought, so I must have been with you somehow."

"You can do that? Pop in and out?"

"I guess. I'm not certain, but I know things that I only could if I'd been with you. Yesterday we had lunch with Trevor. He had a burger and we had a seafood salad. A woman Trev knows came over to our table and sat in his lap. He was polite but pushed her off, and the whole time we were thinking how satisfying it would be to pull her fake platinum hair out by the roots."

Now it was my turn to frown. "You're right. I think maybe I need to talk to Chan again." Chan, the magic shop owner, seemed to know what was going on between Alyson and me a lot better than I did. "I thought at some point we'd just get slapped back together. I imagined it as a single move, not a gradual assimilation."

"You know we can't merge for good unless you decide to stay," Alyson pointed out.

I tucked my bottom lip into my mouth and nibbled on a corner. "Chan did say that."

"And I know you've been considering it," Alyson added.

"I have," I admitted.

"Not surprising. We love it here. Even though you only lived here for two years, in your heart, Cutter's Cove is home."

I acknowledged the truth in that. "It *is* home and I do love it, but I have a job and a boyfriend to consider."

"A job you've tired of and a boyfriend you know you won't miss if you never see him again. A boyfriend you were thinking of breaking up with anyway."

Alyson really could read my mind. It was a little disconcerting, even if she *was* part of me. "Can we change the subject?"

"Sure." Alyson waved her hand in a panoramic gesture. "Don't forget to take the photo for Mom.'

"Hang on a sec." I got up and jogged into the house, where I'd left my Nikon. I could have taken the photo with my phone, but this sunrise deserved special treatment. I took dozens of photos, changing lenses, filters, and perspectives several times. Mom would have a lot of good options to choose from. It was too bad she'd gone in to get dressed before the big show had begun.

I think one of the reason I'd gone into graphic design was because of my love of working with shapes, colors, angles, and light. Mom was an artist both as a hobby and a part-time profession, so I supposed I'd inherited my artistic instincts from her. She was a genius with a paintbrush, but I'd found the medium I enjoyed the most was photography. Catching the perfect image at just the right time and in the right light truly was an art form not everyone understand.

In addition to taking photographs, I enjoyed creating images, layering colors and shapes until I had an image almost as lifelike as an actual photograph. I used those images to enhance the ads I created, which had made my skill as a graphic artist a widely sought-after commodity. I supposed if I did move to Cutter's Cove permanently, I could convert Mom's art studio in the attic into a photography studio in which I could create and sell my photographs and graphic images on the internet.

"Do you think the sky looks like this from the other side?" Alyson asked as she leaned her head against her chin while enjoying the colorful show taking place over the sea.

"You mean if you were in a plane looking down on the clouds from above?"

"I guess."

"I've been in a plane during cloudy sunsets. I can't say I've ever experienced a sunrise blanketed by clouds. The sunsets I've seen from the air were colorful, although nothing like this. I guess we'd have to ask a pilot who flies a lot. It's an interesting question."

Alyson floated over to the chair Mom had vacated and sat down. "I keep thinking about the girl in your dream. I feel as if we should be able to connect with her if she's dead."

"Maybe if we find the grave we'll be able to connect."

"So, we *are* going to look for it?" Alyson asked.

Coming to a decision, I nodded. "We're absolutely going to look for it."

By the time I went upstairs, showered, and dressed, Trevor had arrived. The pizza parlor was closed on Mondays, so I assumed he planned to spend the day with us, as he had every Monday since I'd been here. He'd seemed happy to go along with whatever I'd wanted to do, so I hoped he'd be willing to help me research and attempt to locate the gravesite I'd been dreaming of.

"Was an effort made to find Naomi when she first disappeared?" Mom asked as she set the food on the table and we dug in.

I took a sip of my juice before answering. "I asked Woody to pull the original police file. It was one of Naomi's teachers, not her father, who reported her missing. The teacher, Elena Goldwin, told Darwin Young, the officer who was in charge then who's since retired, that Naomi had missed a whole week of school, which was highly unusual for her. When Ms. Goldwin called the father to see why she was out, he said Naomi was visiting an aunt who'd recently had a baby and needed her help. Ms. Goldwin made a comment about Naomi doing her schoolwork from the aunt's house so she wouldn't get behind, and the father more or less told her to mind her own business and hung up. That was when she called the police and spoke to Officer Young."

"Sounds fishy," Trevor commented as he helped himself to a second serving of pancakes and bacon.

"I agree," Mom said, topping off their coffees. "Did Officer Young follow up?"

"According to Woody, Office Young went to speak to Naomi's father. It was at that point that he admitted they had argued when he'd come home drunk the weekend before and she'd taken off. He was sure she'd be back when she cooled off a bit, so he hadn't reported her missing. He also admitted Naomi didn't have an aunt, pregnant or otherwise."

"So her jerk of a father killed Naomi and dumped the body," Trevor said.

"Officer Young thought so," I responded, "but he couldn't prove it. Naomi's body was never found and a thorough search of the house, the property, and outbuildings surrounding the house, didn't turn up blood or any other physical evidence. Naomi's father insisted he hadn't laid a hand on his daughter, and Officer Young had no way to prove he had."

"Were other suspects considered?" Mom asked.

I nodded. "A few. In my opinion, and in Woody's, the case was dropped much too quickly because Young was so sure the father was guilty. I'm not saying that if Naomi is dead her father didn't do it; I'm just saying there wasn't a lot of effort put into finding alternatives."

Trevor refilled his glass of milk and took a sip. "Okay, so Officer Young didn't look at a lot of other suspects, but he did look at a few. Who?"

"Three other people were interviewed. The first was a boy she went out with earlier in the week. Her father didn't allow her to date, but he'd gone on an overnight fishing charter up north, and Naomi used his absence as an opportunity to go out and have some fun. The boy's name was Greg Dalton. He was a high school jock who could have dated pretty much anyone he wanted. Given the huge gap in social ranking between Dalton and Naomi, it was widely assumed by the other students Officer Young spoke to that he'd only asked her out as some sort of a joke or dare. Officer Young was never able to confirm it, but he did learn from one of Dalton's ex-girlfriends that anyone who went out with the star receiver on the football team had better be prepared to put out. The consensus was that if Naomi refused to sleep with him, he wouldn't have taken it well."

Trevor frowned. "So Dalton might have killed her for not sleeping with him?"

"He might not have been willing to take no for an answer and forced himself on her, killing her accidentally during the course of the rape. Office

Young was never able to prove it, and Dalton never admitted to any wrongdoing, so the idea never went anywhere."

Mom forked a strawberry. "That poor girl. It sounds like she lived a dark, painful life. If she's alive, if she did simply run away, I hope she found happiness."

I hoped that as well, but somehow, I didn't think this story was going to have a happy ending.

"Who else did Officer Young look at?" Trevor asked.

"Two other men in the community. One was Frank Joplin, a homeless man who hung out by the wharf. The weekend before Naomi first missed school, she was seen talking to him near Hammerhead Beach. Connie Arnold, a classmate of Naomi and a very good friend of Greg, was the person who reported witnessing the conversation. Officer Young suspected the girl was just trying to give him another suspect to help Greg out, but he tracked down Oswald and spoke to him anyway."

"And…?" Mom asked.

"He told Officer Young he didn't remember speaking to the girl, but he noted that Oswald was wasted most of the time and didn't seem to remember much of anything. It was Officer Young's conclusion that Oswald was probably not responsible for any wrongdoing in connection to Naomi's disappearance, but he was never able to confirm he wasn't involved either because he couldn't provide an alibi."

"And the other man?" Mom asked. She was literally sitting on the edge of her chair.

I took a sip of water and continued. "The second local man to be interviewed was Jeffrey Kline, a music teacher for the middle school who also did private lessons. It seems that Kline and Naomi struck up a friendship while she was in the school. She desperately wanted to study music, but her dad wouldn't allow it, so, based on what Kline told Young, he would sometimes give her a piano lesson either before or after school. After she moved on to high school, Naomi would go to his home from time to time when she could sneak away. Kline assured Officer Young that nothing inappropriate went on, but a few of Naomi's peers stated there was a rumor that he was actually trading his services as a teacher for sexual favors. Officer Young wasn't able to prove it one way or another, and Kline left Cutter's Cove shortly after Naomi disappeared."

"Do we know where he is now?" Trevor asked.

"He lives on the peninsula about four hours north of here." Once I'd finished disseminating the information I'd gathered, we fell into an introspective silence. Whether Naomi was murdered or simply ran away, it was hard to deal with the fact that this poor girl had suffered so much during the sixteen years she'd lived in town. Woody hadn't been a cop when all this went down, so all he really had were the notes Darwin Young left behind. Based on what we knew, it didn't sound like the girl had a single happy day in her seemingly short life.

"What happened to the father?" Trevor asked. "Does he still live here?"

I nodded. "He does, in the same house he lived in with Naomi. He still fishes for a living and spends most of his free time in one of the local bars."

"Seems if he were guilty he would have left the area," Mom suggested.

I tilted my head just a bit. "Perhaps. We don't know for certain that Naomi is dead, and even if she is, we don't know that her father was responsible. It would seem however that if he were guilty of a brutal crime, he would want to move on, but a lot of killers stay put in the same place where the murders they carried out were committed."

The room fell into a momentary silence as we tried to deal with a possible killer still living in the community.

"What about the mother?" Mom asked. "You said she was in a mental health facility when Naomi went missing. Is she still alive?"

"Yes. And after a couple of years of therapy and a steady drug regimen, she seems to be much better. Collins divorced her after Naomi disappeared, and she's since remarried. She lives about an hour south of Cutter's Cove. She, along with a few people who went to school with Naomi and still live in town, are on my list of people to interview. I planned to start with what I have today."

"I'm totally in," Trevor said.

Tucker let out a single sharp bark and Sunny ran around the room, chasing Shadow. It seemed I had a sleuthing team to help me with what I was sure was going to be a complex case to unravel. Now all we needed was Mac and her tech know-how and we'd hopefully have everything we needed to accomplish what Officer Young had been unable to years ago.

Kathi's Favorite Summer Recipes

Easy Picnic Potato Salad
Strawberry Jell-O Salad
Hobo Packs for the grill or campfire
Fudge Sundae Pie
Mocha Ice Cream Pie
Strawberry Angel Cake
Strawberry Champagne Cheesecake

Easy Picnic Potato Salad

6 medium potatoes, boiled and skinned (Boil in skin until very done. When skin begins to crack, rinse with cool water and then peel skin away; it should peel very easily.)
8 hard-boiled eggs (I sometimes use up to 12)
2 cups mayonnaise
1 cup hot dog relish (yellow)

Combine in large bowl. Season to taste. I use Lawry's salt, pepper, and paprika.

Strawberry Jell-O Salad

2 small boxes strawberry Jell-O
16 oz. (about 2 cups) sliced strawberries
1 cup chopped walnuts
16 oz. sour cream

Mix:
1 small box strawberry Jell-O (made per directions on box)
1 pint (16 oz.) sliced strawberries
1 cup chopped walnuts (add more if you really like nuts)

Pour into bottom of 9 x 13 glass baking dish. Chill until set (about 2 hours).

After first layer is set:
Spread 16-oz. container of sour cream over the top (do not use low fat). Chill for 30 minutes.

Make second small box of strawberry Jell-O according to directions. Carefully pour or ladle the Jell-O on top of sour cream layer; be careful when placing this layer on top or you'll mess up the sour cream. Chill for 2 hours.

Hobo Packs for the grill or campfire

Anyone who has ever gone camping has probably made a hobo pack. There are as many variations as there are people making them. Basically, you place your meat and veggies in a large piece of heavy-duty foil and then place the foil in the coals of a hot-burning wood or charcoal fire. You can make many different variations, but my favorite is the basic meat-and-potatoes kind.

On a large piece of heavy-duty foil, place:

seasoned hamburger patty
thinly sliced potato
thinly sliced carrot
sliced onion
asparagus spears

Wrap the foil around the food (I double wrap) and place into the coals of the fire, turning occasionally. Cook until desired doneness (this depends on the amount of food and the temperature of the fire).

You can also do this with steak, chicken, fish, and any type of veggie you like.

Fudge Sundae Pie

Crust:
¼ cup light corn syrup
2 tbs. brown sugar
3 tbs. butter
2½ cups Rice Krispies cereal

Combine corn syrup, brown sugar, and butter in saucepan. Cook over medium heat until it boils. Pour over Rice Krispies. Stir together and then press into buttered pie plate.

Topping:
½ cup peanut butter
½ cup chocolate fudge sauce
3 tbs. corn syrup
(Note: I often make extra topping and pile it on thick. It's up to you.)

Mix together and spread half on piecrust. Layer in softened ice cream. I use vanilla, but coffee or chocolate work as well. Spread other half of topping over top.

Freeze for 2–3 hours.

Mocha Ice Cream Pie

Melt:
3 tbs. butter in sauce pan

Add:
2 tbs. brown sugar
¼ cup corn syrup

Cook on medium heat until it boils. Pour over 2½ cups Rice Krispies cereal.

Press into buttered pie plate.

Mix together:
½ cup caramel sauce
½ cup peanut butter
3 tbs. corn syrup

Spread half on piecrust. Cover with softened coffee ice cream. Spread other half of sauce mixture on top.

Freeze for 2–3 hours.

Strawberry Angel Cake

Make angel food cake according to directions on box; bake in angel flute cake pan. Cool completely. Cut top off about one-inch down. Scoop out middle, leaving adequate cake on sides.

Mix together:
1 small box strawberry Jell-O, made according to directions and chilled until set
⅓ small (8 oz.) Cool Whip
⅔ pint (16 oz.) fresh strawberries, cut up small

Fill cake with Jell-O mixture; there will be some mixture left in most cases. Replace cake "lid" that was set aside. Frost with remaining Cool Whip. Garnish with remaining whole strawberries.

Strawberry Champagne Cheesecake

1 cup champagne or other sparkling wine
2 cups chocolate graham cracker crumbs (about 14 whole crackers)
2 cups sugar, divided
½ cup butter, melted
1 cup sliced fresh strawberries
3 pkg. (8 oz. each) cream cheese, softened
½ cup sweetened condensed milk
2 tbs. cornstarch
2 eggs, lightly beaten
2 egg yolks

Topping:
20 fresh strawberries, hulled
⅓ cup milk chocolate chips
1 tsp. shortening, divided
⅓ cup white baking chips
1 cup heavy whipping cream
¼ cup confectioner's sugar

Place champagne in a small saucepan. Bring to a boil; cook until liquid is reduced to about ¼ cup, about 8 minutes. Set aside to cool.

In a small bowl, combine the cracker crumbs, ½ cup sugar, and butter. Press onto the bottom and 1½ in. up the sides of a greased 9-in. springform pan; set aside. Arrange sliced strawberries over the bottom.

In a large bowl, beat cream cheese and remaining sugar until smooth. Beat in the sweetened condensed milk, cornstarch, and reduced champagne. Add eggs and egg yolks; beat on low speed until just combined. Pour over strawberries. Place pan on a baking sheet.

Bake at 325 degrees for 55–60 minutes or until center is almost set. Cool on a wire rack for 10 minutes. Carefully run a knife around the edge of the pan to loosen; cool 1 hour longer. Refrigerate overnight.

Remove sides of springform pan. For topping, wash strawberries and gently pat with paper towels until completely dry. Slice and arrange over cheesecake. In a microwave, melt chocolate chips and ½ tsp. shortening; stir until smooth. Drizzle over strawberries. Repeat melting and drizzling with white baking chips and remaining shortening.

In a small bowl, beat cream until it begins to thicken. Add confectioner's sugar; beat until soft peaks form. Serve cheesecake with whipped cream.

Books by Kathi Daley

Come for the murder, stay for the romance.

Zoe Donovan Cozy Mystery:

Halloween Hijinks
The Trouble With Turkeys
Christmas Crazy
Cupid's Curse
Big Bunny Bump-off
Beach Blanket Barbie
Maui Madness
Derby Divas
Haunted Hamlet
Turkeys, Tuxes, and Tabbies
Christmas Cozy
Alaskan Alliance
Matrimony Meltdown
Soul Surrender
Heavenly Honeymoon
Hopscotch Homicide
Ghostly Graveyard
Santa Sleuth
Shamrock Shenanigans
Kitten Kaboodle
Costume Catastrophe
Candy Cane Caper
Holiday Hangover
Easter Escapade
Camp Carter

Trick or Treason
Reindeer Roundup
Hippity Hoppity Homicide
Firework Fiasco
Henderson House – *August 2018*

Zimmerman Academy The New Normal
Ashton Falls Cozy Cookbook

Tj Jensen Paradise Lake Mysteries by Henery Press:

Pumpkins in Paradise
Snowmen in Paradise
Bikinis in Paradise
Christmas in Paradise
Puppies in Paradise
Halloween in Paradise
Treasure in Paradise
Fireworks in Paradise
Beaches in Paradise – *July 2018*

Whales and Tails Cozy Mystery:

Romeow and Juliet
The Mad Catter
Grimm's Furry Tail
Much Ado About Felines
Legend of Tabby Hollow
Cat of Christmas Past
A Tale of Two Tabbies
The Great Catsby
Count Catula
The Cat of Christmas Present

A Winter's Tail
The Taming of the Tabby
Frankencat
The Cat of Christmas Future
Farewell to Felines
A Whisker in Time – *September 2018*

Writers' Retreat Mystery:
First Case
Second Look
Third Strike
Fourth Victim
Fifth Night
Sixth Cabin
Seventh Chapter - *August 2018*

Rescue Alaska Paranormal Mystery:
Finding Justice
Finding Answers
Finding Courage - *September 2018*

A Tess and Tilly Mystery:
The Christmas Letter
The Valentine Mystery
The Mother's Day Mishap
The Halloween House – *July 2018*

Haunting by the Sea:
Homecoming by the Sea
Secrets by the Sea – *June 2018*

Sand and Sea Hawaiian Mystery:
Murder at Dolphin Bay
Murder at Sunrise Beach
Murder at the Witching Hour
Murder at Christmas
Murder at Turtle Cove
Murder at Water's Edge
Murder at Midnight

Seacliff High Mystery:
The Secret
The Curse
The Relic
The Conspiracy
The Grudge
The Shadow
The Haunting

Road to Christmas Romance:
Road to Christmas Past

USA Today best-selling author Kathi Daley lives in beautiful Lake Tahoe with her husband Ken. When she isn't writing, she likes spending time hiking the miles of desolate trails surrounding her home. She has authored more than seventy-five books in eight series, including Zoe Donovan Cozy Mysteries, Whales and Tails Island Mysteries, Sand and Sea Hawaiian Mysteries, Tj Jensen Paradise Lake Series, Writers' Retreat Southern Seashore Mysteries, Rescue Alaska Paranormal Mysteries, and Seacliff High Teen Mysteries. Find out more about her books at **www.kathidaley.com**

Stay up to date:
Newsletter, *The Daley Weekly* **http://eepurl.com/NRPDf**
Webpage – **www.kathidaley.com**
Facebook at Kathi Daley Books –
www.facebook.com/kathidaleybooks
Kathi Daley Books Group Page –
https://www.facebook.com/groups/569578823146850/
E-mail – **kathidaley@kathidaley.com**
Twitter at Kathi Daley@kathidaley –
https://twitter.com/kathidaley
Amazon Author Page –
https://www.amazon.com/author/kathidaley
BookBub – **https://www.bookbub.com/authors/kathi-daley**
Pinterest – **http://www.pinterest.com/kathidaley/**